PENGUIN ● CLASSICS

THE GEORGICS

ADVISORY EDITOR: BETTY RADICE

PUBLIUS VERGILIUS MARO was born in 70 B.C. near Mantua in Cisalpine Gaul, the north of Italy, where his parents owned a farm. He had a good education and went to perfect it in Rome. There he came under the influence of Epicureanism and later joined an Epicurean colony on the Gulf of Naples where he was based for the rest of his life. In 42 B.C. he began to write the *Eclogues*, which he completed in 37 B.C., the year in which he accompanied Horace to Brindisi. The *Georgics* were finished in 29 B.C., and he devoted the rest of his life to the composition of the *Aeneid*. In his last year he started on a journey to Greece; he fell ill at Megara and returned to Italy, but he died in 19 B.C. on reaching Brindisi.

L. P. WILKINSON was born in 1907 and educated at Charterhouse and King's College, Cambridge, where he was Chancellor's Classical Medallist in 1930; he was made a Fellow of the College in 1932. He was successively Lecturer in Classics, Reader in Latin Literature and Brereton Reader in Classics in the University of Cambridge, where from 1958 until 1974 he was Orator. His other publications include *Horace and his Lyric Poetry*, *Ovid Recalled* (abridged as *Ovid Surveyed*, 1962), *Golden Latin Artistry*, *The Georgics of Virgil*, *The Roman Experience*, *Classical Attitudes to Modern Issues* and the words for Benjamin Britten's *Cantata Misericordium*. L. P. Wilkinson died in 1985.

VIRGIL

THE GEORGICS

Translated
into English Verse
with Introduction and Notes
by
L. P. WILKINSON

PENGUIN BOOKS

TO
Guy Lee

PENGUIN BOOKS

Published by the Penguin Group
Penguin Books Ltd, 27 Wrights Lane, London W8 5TZ, England
Penguin Putnam Inc., 375 Hudson Street, New York, New York 10014, USA
Penguin Books Australia Ltd, Ringwood, Victoria, Australia
Penguin Books Canada Ltd, 10 Alcorn Avenue, Toronto, Ontario, Canada M4V 3B2
Penguin Books (NZ) Ltd, 182–190 Wairau Road, Auckland 10, New Zealand

Penguin Books Ltd, Registered Offices: Harmondsworth, Middlesex, England

This translation first published 1982
10

Copyright © L. P. Wilkinson, 1982
All rights reserved

Printed in England by Clays Ltd, St Ives plc
Set in Linotron Bembo

Contents

Preface

For the introductions and notes accompanying this translation I have naturally often had recourse to my book *The Georgics of Virgil* (Cambridge University Press, 1969; paperback edition 1978), in particular borrowing some of the illustrative quotations from there; and I have been helped by reviewers of that book, notably Erich Burck (*Gnomon* 42, 1970, pp. 768–76) and Brooks Otis (*Phoenix* 26, 1972, pp. 40–62). Any student of the *Georgics* must be indebted to the work of these two, and also particularly to K. Büchner's monumental article *Vergilius Maro* in the *Real-Enzyklopädie* and F. Klingner's running commentary *Virgils Georgica* (1963). It has been most helpful to have the commentaries of W. Richter (1957) and R. D. Williams (1979), but much profit and pleasure can still be derived from that of T. E. Page (1898), not to mention the standard edition of Conington–Nettleship–Haverfield. Our standard text is now R. A. B. Mynors (Oxford Classical Text), 2nd edition, 1972.

The *Georgics* have been ploughed and cross-ploughed by verse translators in the past half-century. The version of C. Day Lewis is outstanding for liveliness and for felicitous phrasing (apart from a few lapses into inappropriate slang). But his loose metre, almost *vers libre*, hardly allowed of an attempt such as I have made to give some idea of the *movement* of Virgil's verse. Four blank verse translations also have considerable merits: those of R. C. Trevelyan (1944), L. A. S. Jermyn (1947), the American S. P. Bovie (1956) and K. R. Mackenzie (1969). Dryden's version in heroic couplets (1697), still a delight to read, was reissued in 1981 with the Latin text (ed. A. Elliott) by the Mid Northumberland Arts Group. My practice has been to make my own version and then consult the others. Inevitably there have proved to be coincidences of phrasing, but also from time to time I have gratefully helped myself to a word, while consciously abstaining from appropriating felicities so original as to deserve to have their copyright respected. A note about my translation faces the first page of it. The notes at the end of the book are mainly intended to clarify the meaning of words or phrases in the translation.

I am most grateful to my friend and colleague Guy Lee for

making many valuable suggestions – most of which I have accepted to my advantage, a few rejected at my peril – and indeed for much help and encouragement over the years. I am glad to be able to dedicate the book to him.

L. P. W.   *July 1981*

Select Bibliography
MAINLY IN ENGLISH

Text
MYNORS, R. A. B., Oxford Classical Text, 2nd edn, 1972.

Text and Commentary
CONINGTON, J., NETTLESHIP, H., and HAVERFIELD, F., *Vergil*, vol. I, Bell, 1898.
HUXLEY, H. H., Books I and 4 (for schools), Methuen, 1963.
PAGE, T. E., Macmillan, 1898.
RICHTER, W. (in German), Hueber, 1957.
WILLIAMS, R. D., Macmillan, 1979.

Text and Translation
DE SAINT-DENIS (in French, with introduction and notes), Budé, 1956.
DRYDEN, J., 1698, ed. A. Elliott, Mid Northumberland Arts Group, 1981.
FAIRCLOUGH, H. R., with *Eclogues* and *Aeneid* 1–6, Loeb, 1932.

Translation (verse)
BOVIE, S. P., *Georgics*, University of Chicago, 1956.
DAY LEWIS, C., *Georgics*, Cape, 1940; with *Eclogues* and *Aeneid*, Oxford Paperbacks, 1966.
JERMYN, L. A. S., *The Singing Farmer*, Blackwell, 1947.
MACKENZIE, K. R., *The Georgics*, The Folio Society, 1969.
TREVELYAN, R. C., The *Eclogues* and the *Georgics*, 1944.

Books
ABBE, E., *The Plants of Virgil's Georgics*, Cornell University, 1965.
BILLIARD, R., *L'agriculture dans l'antiquité d'après les Géorgiques de Virgile*, Boccard, Paris, 1928.
BOYLE, A. J. (ed.), *Virgil's Ascraean Song, Ramus*, vol. 8, I, Aureal Publications, 1979.
FRASER, H. M., *Beekeeping in Antiquity*, University of London, 1931.
KEIGHTLEY, T., *Notes on the Bucolics and Georgics of Virgil*, Whittaker, 1846.

KLINGNER, F., *Virgils Georgica* (in German), Artemis, Zürich, 1963.

MILES, G. B., *Virgil's Georgics: A New Interpretation*, Berkeley, 1980.

NITCHIE, E., *Virgil and the English Poets*, dissertation, Columbia, 1919.

OTIS, B., *Virgil: a Study in Civilized Poetry*, Oxford University Press, 1963.

PUTNAM, M. C. J., *Virgil's Poem of the Earth*, Princeton University, 1979.

ROYDS, T. F., *The Beasts, Birds and Bees of Virgil*, Blackwell, 1914.

SARGEAUNT, J., *The Trees, Shrubs and Plants of Virgil*, Blackwell, 1920.

SELLAR, W. Y., *Roman Poets of the Augustan Age*, vol. 1: *Virgil*, 3rd edn, Oxford University Press, 1897.

WHITE, K. D., *Roman Agriculture*, Thames and Hudson, 1970.

WILKINSON, L. P., *The Georgics of Virgil*, Cambridge University Press, 1969; paperback edn 1978.

Articles and Reviews

ANDERSON, W. B., 'Gallus and the Fourth Georgic', *Classical Quarterly*, 1933, pp. 36–45, 73.

GRIFFIN, J., 'The Fourth Georgic, Virgil and Rome', *Greece and Rome*, 1979, pp. 60–80.

GRIFFIN, J., 'Haec super arvorum cultu', *Classical Review*, 1981, pp. 23–37 (review of some recent works on the *Georgics*).

JERMYN, L. A. S., 'Weather-signs in Virgil', *Greece and Rome*, 1951, pp. 23–37, 49–59.

MUSTARD, W. P., 'Virgil's *Georgics* and the British Poets', *American Journal of Philology*, 1908, pp. 1–31.

OTIS, B., 'A New Study of the *Georgics*' (extended review of L. P. Wilkinson, *The Georgics of Virgil*), *Phoenix*, 1972, pp. 42–62.

SEGAL, C., 'Orpheus and the Fourth Georgic', *American Journal of Philology*, 1966, pp. 307–25.

WILKINSON, L. P., 'Virgil's Theodicy', *Classical Quarterly*, 1963, pp. 73–84.

WILLIAMS, R. D., *Virgil: Greece and Rome* (New Surveys of the Classics), 1967.

General Introduction

As this is an introduction to a translation, it does not assume in the reader any knowledge of Latin. Line references throughout are based on the Latin text. They are given at ten-line intervals of the translation.

NATURE OF THE POEM

The four Books of Virgil's *Georgics* are unique: they do not conform to any recognized class of poetry. Ostensibly indeed the poem is 'didactic': it teaches about farming. But this should deceive no one today, any more than it deceived Seneca, who within a century of the poet's death remarked almost casually in a letter that Virgil was more interested in perfect expression than perfect truth and wrote not to teach farmers but to delight readers (86.15). We can tell that the poem is not technically didactic because it ignores many subjects about which a farmer would have to be informed, and fails to give detailed instructions without which some of the precepts could not be applied. Few working farmers would be readers of poetry; and in any case there were more serviceable prose manuals available. It is however didactic in the sense that it asserts moral principles, supports political attitudes, and implies philosophical and religious views, as will be indicated below. To a large extent the farmer stands for man in general.

But before dealing with the poem as such it may be desirable to say something of its background – biographical, literary, political and social, religious and philosophical, and agricultural.

LIFE AND WORKS OF VIRGIL

Much of what we are told about Virgil's life in the ancient biographies and commentaries seems to have been gleaned from his own works, sometimes taking what he says too literally, or assuming an allegory where none perhaps exists. On the other hand, since for his last twenty years he was a famous man, and since we know from references that his friends and acquaintances left on record information about his character and ways,[1] anything we have no good reason to suspect is probably true. Thus our ultimate authority for his being in speech slow and almost like an uneducated man is Melissus, who was in the household of his patron Maecenas. At the same time we may accept the evidence of Julius Montanus that verses of his that seemed empty and flat when read by others were made effective by his own voice, expression and gesture.[2] The parallel of Tennyson comes to mind.

We possess also the so-called *Appendix Virgiliana*, consisting of poems attributed to his early years. He must indeed have composed poems in those years; but it is now generally believed that, with the exception of two or three short pieces,[3] the *Appendix* consists of later compositions, partly deliberate fakes, partly works of others mistakenly included.

Publius Virgilius (or Vergilius) Maro was born on 15 October 70 B.C. near Mantua (Mantova), a city in what was then a Roman Province, Gallia Cisalpina ('Gaul this side of the Alps'), the wide plain watered by the river Eridanus or Padus (the Po). The Mincius, flowing down gently from Lake Benacus (Garda) to the Po, widened, as it still does, into a lagoon outside the city walls. Virgil's father, said to have been a farmer, was apparently well enough off to be able to send him, after schooling at Cremona, for higher education to Mediolanum (Milan), the chief cultural centre of the area, and then to Rome for the rhetorical education which any young man with ambitions underwent.[4] The story goes that he was unsuccessful in the only case he pleaded, which is consistent with the tradition that he was exceptionally shy.[5] But at least he could profit by the stylistic part of the course: his verse shows an easy and unobtrusive mastery of the rhetorical 'period'. When he was twenty, Roman citizenship was extended to the part of the province north of the Po, 'Transpadane Gaul', which included Mantua. He thus became a Roman citizen.

At Rome he came under the influence of Epicureanism, a

1. Aulus Gellius 17.10.7.
2. Suetonius, *Vita* 16; 29.
3. *Catalepton* 5, 8 and perhaps 10.
4. Suetonius, *Vita* 6–7; *De Grammaticis* 20; Servius, *Vita*.
5. Suetonius, *Vita* 11.

philosophy which was having a vogue in educated circles (see p. 27). He must have felt the overwhelming impact of the great poem expounding it, Lucretius' *On the Nature of Things*, which was beginning to circulate when he was about sixteen years old. At all events he threw up everything to go and join an Epicurean colony run by one Siro on the Gulf of Naples (Neapolis or Parthenope). A charming poem in the *Appendix*, *Catalepton* 5, blending enthusiasm with humour and a touch of wistfulness, describes his feelings on this occasion:

> Away with you, hollow boomings of the rhetoricians, windbag words inflated in no Attic style; and you, Selius and Tarquitius and Varro, stodgy tribe of pedants, away with you, tinkling cymbals of youth. And you, Sextus Sabinus, my dearest dear, good-bye; good-bye now, all you beauties. I am setting sail for the havens of the blest to seek the wise sayings of great Siro, and will redeem my life from all care. Away with you, Muses: yes, you too must go now, I suppose, sweet Muses (for I will confess it, you *have* been sweet) – and yet, do revisit my pages, but discreetly and rarely.

Mantua and its surroundings remained very much in his mind; but for the rest of his life we must think of him as based on Naples, sometimes visiting other places in south Italy such as Tarentum, but only rarely going to Rome. It was at Naples that he was buried and became a legend in the Middle Ages.

What happened to him in the civil war of 49–45 B.C., in which the supporters of Julius Caesar defeated those of Pompey the Great at Pharsalus and elsewhere after Pompey's death, we do not know. The likelihood, especially if he was still a serious Epicurean, is that he took no active part. When he next emerges it is as a mature poet attached to a distinguished man of action and of letters, Asinius Pollio. Another savage civil war, the result of Caesar's murder in 44, had just been concluded when his political heirs, Caesar Octavian (his great-nephew and adoptive son) and Mark Antony, defeated the Republicans under Brutus and Cassius at Philippi in 42. The poems in the collection of ten known as the *Bucolics* or *Eclogues* were composed apparently over the years 42 to 37[1] (what we have bears marks of being a revised edition). He set out, it

1. Taking the completely detachable Eclogue 8.6–13 as being addressed to Pollio, a relic, probably the envoi of an earlier edition, as against G. W. Bowersock, *Harvard Studies in Classical Philology*, 1971, pp. 73–80.

would seem, to provide the Romans with an analogue to Theocritus, a poet from Syracuse in Sicily who, shortly before 270 B.C., joined the cultured establishment at Alexandria of the Ptolemies, Macedonian Greek kings of Egypt. Some of the Idylls of Theocritus are vignettes of rustic life. It was these that attracted Virgil. But even those of the *Eclogues* which are most clearly intended to recall Theocritus (2, 3, 7 and 8) are infused with Virgil's personality. They are more tender and sentimental than their models; Virgil is more involved in the feelings of his rustics, tending indeed to express his own feelings through them. By the time he had finished he had done two things momentous for the future of European literature and art: he had developed Theocritean mime, detached observations of rustic life, into the genre of romantic pastoral poetry, creating the imaginative world which took from him the name of Arcady; and at the same time, seizing on a trait only embryonic in Theocritus, he had introduced real people into pastoral, thus initiating the pastoral allegory of later times.

He first used the pastoral mode for topical purposes when the victors of Philippi proceeded to evict landholders, initially from communities that had sided against them, in favour of their own veterans. Cremona was among the sufferers; and when more land was wanted, its neighbour Mantua began to suffer as well. Eclogue 9 expresses the disillusionment and desperate half-hopes of those threatened or already evicted. In Eclogue 1 the fortune of Tityrus, an elderly peasant who has been reprieved, is contrasted with that of Meliboeus, who has lost everything. Tityrus expresses fulsome gratitude to a godlike youth, obviously Octavian; but in overall effect the poem is a passionate representation of the plight of the dispossessed, a courageous plea. There is no close allegory, but it is difficult to resist the conclusion that Virgil's father (not himself, as later tradition had it) was among the reprieved. Another short poem in the *Appendix*, *Catalepton* 8, expresses his anxiety at this time:

Little house that belonged to Siro and meagre plot (though to that owner even you were riches), to you I commend myself, and these too with me whom I have always loved, if I hear any gloomier news from home, and above all my father. You will now be to him what Mantua and Cremona were before.

At all events, by the time the *Bucolics* were finally published the friend of Antony's former right-hand man Pollio had joined the circle of Octavian's right-hand man Maecenas. There was no disloyalty in this: Antony and Octavian were officially colleagues, and after the reconciliation in the Treaty of Brundisium, negotiated by Pollio and Maecenas in October 40, they were brothers-in-law, for it was sealed by the marriage of Antony to Octavia. It is true that they drifted apart before long, but Pollio broke with Antony and thereafter adopted a neutral attitude.

The ancient biographers Suetonius and Servius say that the *Georgics* was completed in seven years.[1] We do not know when the conception came into Virgil's head – it may have been as early as 39/38 B.C. – but even Book 1, let alone the rest, was apparently influenced by the appearance in 37/36 of Varro's work (see p. 19); and we may take the poem as having been substantially composed over the years 36 to 29. It shares some features with the *Bucolics*, notably sympathetic interest in rustic life and scenes. In both cases that life is idealized, but in very different ways; for whereas in the *Bucolics* rustic tasks receive only casual mention in an 'Arcadian' world of love and song, the *Georgics* proclaims a 'gospel of work'. The Roman Theocritus has become the Roman Hesiod (see pp. 16–18).

By the time the *Georgics* was finished the long and inevitable rivalry between Antony and Octavian had been resolved by the naval battle of Actium in 31 and Antony's suicide at Alexandria in 30. Octavian, whom we will now call Caesar as he is always called in the *Georgics*, was 'sole sir o' the world', soon to be given the title of *princeps* and the name of Augustus. We are told that when, on his triumphant return from the East in 29, he was resting in his progress with an indisposition at Atella, near Naples, Virgil read the poem to him, Maecenas taking over when his voice gave out.[2] Now wholeheartedly committed to Caesar, Virgil was contemplating an epic celebrating his deeds;[3] but in the end he wisely decided to honour him obliquely instead by one celebrating the foundation of Rome's fortunes by his ancestor, the Trojan Aeneas. By 19 B.C. the *Aeneid* was finished in the state in which we have it.

1. Suetonius 25; Servius, *Vita* 2.
2. Suetonius 27.
3. *Georgics* 3.46–8; cf. 16–39.

The poet intended to revise it substantially, but on a visit to the East he was taken ill near Athens, where he met Caesar. He decided to return with him, and died after landing at Brindisi on 20 September. Before leaving Italy he had instructed his friend and literary executor the poet Varius to burn his manuscript if anything happened to him, but his wishes were overruled by Caesar.[1] Flawed though it is in some respects, the *Aeneid* must be regarded as his masterpiece; but it lacks the finished perfection of the *Georgics*, which it has for too long been allowed to overshadow.

LITERARY BACKGROUND OF THE GEORGICS

Roman literature began as translation from the Greek and shaded into brilliant adaptation, as of Menander's comedies by Terence. Then, in most of Catullus for instance, we encounter originality such as we expect of a poet today. But the desire to emulate, appropriate or acclimatize Greek writers remained. In the *Bucolics* Virgil took his cue, with skilful use of reminiscences, from Theocritus, that outstanding poet of Alexandria who for some reason seems previously to have been overlooked (see p. 14). In the *Georgics* he was inspired by another outstanding Greek poet, Hesiod, who had at one time (unaccountably, to our way of thinking) been spoken of in the same breath as Homer. Hesiod flourished about 700 B.C. in Boeotia, the country north-west of Attica whose chief town was Thebes. He wrote in the dactylic hexameter verse used also by Homer. Two of his poems are extant today, the *Works and Days* and the *Generations of the Gods* (*Theogonia*), and it was the first that attracted Virgil. Of its 800 lines, less than a third (383–617) deal with the farmer's year, and they are mainly confined to the growing of cereals. To categorize the *Works and Days* any more precisely than as 'a didactic and admonitory medley' (Sinclair) would be misleading. As to subject, the essence is conveyed by 'Justice and Work' (Mazon). The poem is addressed to an individual, an unjust brother – a lead followed by Virgil in so far as he normally addresses the reader in the singular whereas the other agricultural writers used the plural.

Hesiod had had a great revival in third-century Alexandria, in

1. Suetonius 35; 39–41.

the highly sophisticated literary circle of Callimachus. His honest water refreshed a generation cloyed with excessive draughts of Homeric-type wine. Jaded palates are apt to rediscover virtue in the archaic, and to some extent the virtue is likely to be genuine. In Hesiod we find forthright archaic vigour, and also a talent for vivid description, as in his pictures of summer and winter (reminiscent to us of Breughel), which Homer could not have bettered (*Works and Days* 582–96; 504–53).

During Virgil's boyhood there arose in the West, which under Roman influence was rapidly becoming hellenized and sophisticated, a literary movement now known, from a Greek word casually thrown out by Cicero in a letter, as the 'Neoteric' (Modernist). I say 'the West' rather than 'Rome' because of the interesting fact that one of the leaders of the movement, Valerius Cato, came from Milan, where Virgil received his higher education, and several more of its chief poets (including Virgil himself, Catullus, their friend Cinna, Varro of Atax, Quintilius Varus and Cornelius Gallus) were from north or west of the Po, from a region of Cisalpine (and even Transalpine) Gaul not yet officially incorporated even in Italy. All, of course, gravitated to Rome. Virgil's first patron Asinius Pollio may also be reckoned a member: indeed it may have been in such circles that the two met.

The literary hero of this movement was Callimachus. Like him, the Modernists were tired of bombastic, derivative epic poetry, and cultivated subtleties of diction, allusion and wit which were best appreciated within the compass of short poems. Different writers were affected by the movement in different ways. Virgil and his younger contemporary Horace clearly derived much benefit from it in the matter of artistic refinements; as to thought, with the dawning of what became Augustan ideals, they passed into, or rather created, another phase. Virgil's original interest in Hesiod may have been a Neoteric inheritance from Callimachean Alexandria. The imagined consecration of Gallus by Linus on behalf of the Muses at Eclogue 6.64–73 is explicitly inspired by Hesiod's description at the beginning of the *Theogony* of his own mystical experience of meeting with the Muses on Mount Helicon; and there are reminiscences of him elsewhere in the *Bucolics*. But in the *Georgics*, although a famous passage in Book 2 culminates in the line (176) '[I] sing the song of Ascra through the towns of

Rome' (Ascra was Hesiod's home village), we find specific influence from his work only in Book 1, where lines 43–203 correspond, though not at all closely, to his 'Works', 204–350 to his 'Days'. Sometimes a turn of phrase is purposely reminiscent of him; sometimes the inclusion of archaistic matter is a bow in his direction. But Hesiod's main significance for Virgil is of a more general kind. The idea of addressing a small independent farmer who works for himself is Hesiodic, and so is the insistence on the moral value of hard work. The gods have put sweat in the path of virtue; idleness is a vice; work brings property, and property wins self-respect and respect from others. Such ideas, now long rooted in western, especially puritan, mentality, are well exemplified in Longfellow's *The Village Blacksmith*.

A literary feature of the Hellenistic age (323–146 B.C.) was the appearance of 'metaphrasts', versifiers of the prose treatises of others. One of the better ones, Aratus, links Hesiod with Virgil. His *Phaenomena*, on the stars, with an appendix on weather-signs, was much admired by the Callimacheans for its austerity and its elegant hexameter verse. Translated into Latin by Cicero and Ovid among others, it was respected as a didactic poem until consigned to obscurity by the discoveries of Copernicus and Galileo. Following Hesiod, Aratus has a hymn to Zeus as prelude, and also a description of descending mythical ages of men, Gold, Silver and Bronze (96–136). But most of the poem is a catalogue. Here and there, especially in the weather-signs, it is enlivened with picturesque detail, which may have shown Virgil how effective this could be. The lost *Georgics* and *Beekeeping* by a more pedestrian versifier, Nicander, may also have given him something, for he had the ability to discern the precious jewel in the head of any toad. But he also looked outside the didactic tradition, notably to Pindar for the proem to Book 3 and to Homer, both *Iliad* and *Odyssey*, for the Aristaeus narrative in Book 4.

But infinitely more important, the true inspirer of the poem, was Lucretius, who, though also making use of the works of others in prose and verse, soared above those metaphrasts both in seriousness of purpose and in poetic value. Lucretius could show Virgil, more clearly than Aratus, how a poem expounding scientific matter could, by sheer accumulation of picturesque detail, acquire the qualities of a descriptive one, and how it could also be charged with relevant moral and philosophic fervour. Both hated civil war. Both hated the hectic life of the opulent city. Lucretius escaped into Epicurean philosophy, Virgil into contemplation of country life, both into their art. Temperamentally they were very different – Lucretius an uncompromising rationalist, Virgil an eclectic visionary (see p. 31). But Virgil will often take an idea from Lucretius and adapt it for quite different purposes. Indeed his poem has been described as a submerged dialogue with Lucretius.

Finally, there was a prose writer who had some influence on the *Georgics*, both literary and technical. The eminent scholar and polymath Varro of Reate produced as a nonagenarian in 37/36 his *De Re Rustica*, written as a guide for his wife in the management of a farm he had given her. This, no doubt with Cicero in mind, he cast in literary form, as a dialogue. Among other features his prologue invoking twelve gods of the country and his set pieces eulogizing Italy and country life may have suggested prominent passages in the *Georgics*.[1] In parts of Book 3 Virgil follows him quite closely. But some didactic passages also show how Virgil could elaborate and transform the work of his predecessor. Here is an instance, concerning herdsmen of sheep and goats. Varro[2] has:

In summer they go out to pasture them at daybreak, because the grass, being dewy, is more palatable than at mid-day, when it is drier. When the sun is up they drive them to water, refresh them and so make them keener to feed. About the time of the mid-day heat they drive them under shady rocks and spreading trees to cool down till the day gets milder. In the evening air they feed them again till sunset.

And now Virgil:

> But when glad summer at the Zephyrs' call
> Sends sheep and goats alike to glades and meadows,
> Let us hasten as the morning star appears
> To the cool pastures, while the day is young,
> The grass is gleaming, and on the tender blades
> There still is dew delightful to the herd.
> Then, when the sky's fourth hour has brought their thirst
> To a head, and with incessant dinning drone
> Cicalas burst the bushes, I will lead
> The flocks to drink at wells or standing pools
> Water that runs in troughs of ilex-wood.

1. 1.2.3–8; 2.1–3. *Georgics* 2.136–76; 458–540.
2. 2.2.10–12; *Georgics* 3.322–38.

But in the noonday heat I'll have them seek
A shady valley where some ancient oak
Of Jupiter with venerable trunk
Extends huge branches, or an ilex grove
Thick-planted broods with dark and holy shadow;
Then feed again till the sun sets and drink
Clear water when the evening star is cooling
The air and the moon refreshing the glades with dew,
And calls of birds re-echo, from the shore
The kingfisher's, the warbler's from the thorn.

In so far as Virgil's sources are extant, the way he handled and rearranged the material gives us valuable insights into his poetic purposes.

POLITICAL CLIMATE

In the proem to Book 3, after proclaiming his intention of writing an epic, Virgil continues (40):

Meanwhile however let my Muse pursue
The woods and glades of the Dryads, virgin country,
No soft assignment by your will, Maecenas.

This has naturally been supposed by many to mean that the *Georgics* was undertaken at Maecenas' instigation. But the word here rendered as 'will',. *iussa*, can indicate something milder and more like 'encouragement'. Virgil had used it to describe the role in the genesis of his *Bucolics* played by Pollio, who was certainly not in a position to give him commands. Also this passage, written years after the poem was begun, may mean no more than that Maecenas was urging him to complete it. At any rate, the *Georgics* was certainly a labour of love, as Virgil himself says (3.285): 'captivated I linger lovingly, touring from this to that.' He had already indicated in the *Bucolics* how deeply anxious he was for a revival of farming, for which he had pinned his hopes on Julius Caesar (see p. 24). But although there was clearly need for an end to civil war if the countryside, neglected where not actually devastated, was ever to recover, there is not much evidence of an active Augustan policy of 'back to the land'. The subject was certainly in the air, with social and moral overtones, but *laisser faire* favoured the continuing growth of large estates. We may surmise that, as far as conditions of land-tenure went, the mainspring of the *Georgics* was not political.

But that is not to say that it had no other political implications. The *Georgics* celebrates a land that had been united politically only two generations previously, with the raising of the Italian allies to full Roman citizenship following their successful revolt, known as the Social (i.e. Allies') War, in 89 B.C. Indeed, as we saw, Virgil's own native region had been added only very recently. The historian Polybius, in the second century, had recognized Italy as a geographical unit reaching to the Alps, and the use of Latin for military and diplomatic purposes had long been a unifying factor; but it will have taken time for the Italians to feel themselves really Roman, and the Romans really Italian. The *Georgics* is the great poem of united Italy. Others, including Varro, had praised the variety, fertility, self-sufficiency and temperate climate of that land, and the elder Cato, who wrote an extant treatise on agriculture in the second century, had praised the hardy qualities of its sons. Virgil's famous eulogy of Italy (2.136–76) is a culmination: it adds a new dimension, the association of this land with the greatness of Rome – *Romana per oppida, Romanos triumphos* – and the religion whose Mecca was the Roman Capitol with its temples of Jupiter and Juno (143–50):

> . . .the land is full
> Of teeming fruits and Bacchus' Massic liquor.
> Olives are everywhere and prosperous cattle.
> From here the war-horse comes that charges proudly
> Over the plain; from here your milk-white herds,
> Clitumnus, and the bull, greatest of victims,
> Plunged often in your sacred stream, that lead
> Triumphant Romans to the Capitol.

Virgil, having been brought up in the extreme north, having had experience of Rome, and having spent his adult life in the extreme south, was ideally suited to be the poet of united Italy. Of the Italian geographical names that occur in the *Georgics* – only about thirty – twenty are from the parts he knew best.

The Romano–Italian greatness was shown not only in war, but in works; and the works were not only admirable in their construction, but part of a grandiose landscape (155–64):

> And then the cities,
> So many noble ones raised by our labours,
> So many towns we've piled on precipices,
> And rivers gliding under ancient walls.
> What of the seas, the Upper and the Lower,
> That wash our shores? What of the Great Lakes,
> You, mightiest Larius, and you, Benācus,
> Surging with waves and roaring like the sea?
> What of the harbours and the Lucrine barrage
> And ocean loud with indignation seething
> Where far the baffled Julian waves resound
> And Tyrrhene tides flow channelled into Avernus?

Agrippa's Julian Port with its long mole and the new canal that connected Lake Avernus with the Gulf of Naples has disappeared, like Virgil's own tomb, with the subsidence that has affected that volcanic coast; but the great blocks of ancient 'Cyclopean' masonry on which some of the hill-towns such as Cortona and Segni are based can still be seen, and the Arno still glides beneath ancient walls at Florence and Pisa. And finally there was the breed of men produced by Italy, the anonymous tribesmen and the famous worthies (167–74):

> The same has bred a vigorous race of men,
> Marsians, the Sabine stock, Ligurians
> Inured to hardship, Volscians javelin-armed,
> And heroes, Decii, Marii, Camilli,
> Scipios, stubborn fighters, and you, Caesar,
> Greatest of all, who now victoriously
> In Asia's farthest bounds are fending off
> Unwarlike Indians from our Roman strongholds.

In this passage of exhilarating rhetoric the picture is somewhat idealized. Most of Italy consisted of rough upland pasture exploited for absentee landlords of huge estates by slaves under a bailiff, not by those to whom the poem is addressed: farmers working a smallholding with their own hands. Indeed slavery, the basis of Italian agriculture in general, is, astonishingly, hardly mentioned in the *Georgics*. It is true that there were still parts of Italy in which a farmer was still what Virgil had in mind, a smallholder or tenant (*colonus*), and that these parts included those with which he himself was most familiar, the Po valley and the 'Ager Campanus', the district round Naples which was let to small tenants by the Roman state. Nor must we forget the veterans who were settled on the land of the dispossessed, or whoever they employed to farm it for them. Nevertheless the deliberate exclusion of slavery from the *Georgics* can only be seen as highly significant: the contrast with the contemporary assumptions of Varro, a large landowner, is striking. It is also noteworthy that, however much legend might honour Cincinnatus, who retired from his dictatorship and returned to his plough as soon as the work for which he had been summoned had been done, the social status of the *colonus* had been low in the eyes of recent Roman writers.

In the eulogy discussed above, Italy, the temperate land of 'perpetual spring', is praised as exemplifying the golden mean by contrast with the exotic and dangerous extremes of the fabulous East. In a more concrete way Italian sentiment was consolidated by events that took place while Virgil was composing the *Georgics*. Antony was away in the East, ostensibly if not effectively engaged in pacifying the frontier of the Empire in Asia Minor but in fact dallying dangerously with Cleopatra. There were disquieting rumours that he intended to transfer the capital of the Empire to Alexandria. His colleague Caesar meanwhile was pacifying the West. He and his general Agrippa eliminated Lepidus, the nonentity who was the third in the Triumvirate, and the piratical Sextus Pompeius, last leader of the partisans of his father Pompey the Great. When the breach between Caesar and Antony became open in 32 B.C., though three hundred senators had gone to join Antony, the whole of Italy, whether spontaneously as was claimed or not, swore allegiance town by town to Caesar. It is perhaps to this crisis of anxiety that we should refer Virgil's outburst at the end of the First Georgic (498–501):

> Gods of our fathers, Heroes of our land,
> And Romulus and mother Vesta, guardian
> Of Tuscan Tiber and Roman Palatine,
> Do not prevent at least this youthful prince
> From saving a world in ruins . . .

By the time the *Georgics* was finished, in 29 B.C., Antony was dead, and it was Caesar who was returning in triumph from the eastern frontier. The epilogue of the poem is extremely interesting (4.559 –66):

> This song of the husbandry of crops and beasts
> And fruit-trees I was singing while great Caesar
> Was thundering beside the deep Euphrates
> In war, victoriously for grateful peoples
> Appointing laws and setting his course for Heaven.
> I, Virgil, at that time lay in the lap
> Of sweet Parthenopê, enjoying there
> The studies of inglorious ease, who once
> Dallied in pastoral verse and with youth's boldness
> Sang of you, Tityrus, lazing under a beech-tree.

We note the pride in the Empire and what was to be the Augustan ideal of it as bestowing on the world the Roman rule of law; also the forecast of immortality as reward for the man who would bring this about. But we also note the pride of the humbly born poet who, not without a genial touch of irony, can set his own 'inglorious' (*ignobilis*) life of the spirit, of Epicurean leisure, beside that of the conqueror, and add a reminder of the boldness with which in his youth he had brought home to this same conqueror, the young man whom his Tityrus would always revere as a god, the plight of the evicted Meliboeus.

It was to be expected that in the conflict between the Republicans and the political heirs of Julius Caesar, Antony and Octavian, Virgil should incline to the latter side. Caesar had been, from the time of Virgil's infancy, the popular governor of his province, Cisalpine Gaul. He took steps to extend Roman citizenship to the Transpadanes as soon as he became Dictator. Again, Virgil's mentor Siro was closely associated with Calpurnius Piso, father of Julius' wife Calpurnia. In the Ninth Eclogue (44–50) he speaks of the Julian Star, the comet which appeared during the games held in Julius' honour three months after his death and which was widely believed to be his soul translated to Heaven, as having aroused hope of a revival of agriculture; and the same idea is amplified in the Fifth Eclogue if, as many scholars believe, Daphnis there is meant to suggest Julius. In the *Georgics* he speaks of the sun as pitying Rome on the extinction of Julius (1.466). His entry, early in the thirties, to the circle of Maecenas committed him all the more thereafter to the young Caesar, the future Augustus. The sincerity of his devotion should not be questioned. But he never lost sight of the other side of the coin, the cost in terms of human suffering that the imposition of order involves – the cost, for instance, of Aeneas' having to desert Dido for the furtherance of the destiny of Rome.

In the proem to the Third Georgic we have, a remarkable proclamation of how Virgil conceived of his relationship to the young Caesar. He imagines himself as leading the Muses in triumph from Greek Helicon, not to Rome but to his own native Mantua, and of building there a temple to Caesar. After the example of Pindar, who in the fifth century B.C. sang odes in honour of the victors, some of them kings, in the Olympic and other Greek games, he represents himself as master of ceremonies at Mantuan games; and in describing the building of the temple he adopts Pindaric symbols of poetic architecture. At first he is himself a victor, echoing the claim of the first great Roman poet Ennius (9) and himself bearing the palms of victory in the new games (12; 17–18). But in the account of the temple and its sculptures the imagery of the games melts into that of a Roman Triumph with Caesar as the *triumphator* whose cult statue it will enshrine. On 13–15 August of that year, 29 B.C., Caesar celebrated a triple Triumph, for victories won in Illyricum and elsewhere by his subordinates, and by himself at Actium and Alexandria. A fortnight later he dedicated a temple to The Divine Julius, his adoptive father; and already he was erecting on the Palatine Hill the temple of Apollo, famous for its sculptures, which was to be dedicated a year later. Only the precedent of Pindar prepares us for the astonishing boldness of a poet so confident in his genius that he could associate himself on these terms with a Roman *imperator* in the hour of his Triumph.

The temple of The Divine Julius resulted from a vote of the Senate and People on 1 January 42 recognizing the dead Julius as a god. This was the first time that a man had been so recognized at Rome. Caesar Octavian as his adoptive son thus became 'son of a god'. Italian cities enrolled him among their local divinities, Lares, after his defeat of Sextus Pompeius in 36. The Senate now decreed a quinquennial festival in his name and annual services on his birthday. It was in this almost hysterical atmosphere that Virgil

25

composed the proem to Book 3, and also the probably contemporaneous proem to the whole poem in Book 1, in which, with every extravagance of adulation, he invokes him as one who will presently be a god. To this same period we may attribute his friend Horace's no less adulatory Ode 1.2. The idea of divine honours for rulers had long been familiar in Asiatic, Greek and Punic communities, but had only recently invaded Italy. For dead rulers it was only just assimilable there, for living ones even less easily so. Revulsion at the association of such ideas with the living Julius Caesar had been one of the motives for his assassination. His great-nephew, when he became Augustus, was more cautious: he pertinaciously repressed any deification of himself in the capital, and the flatteries of the poets became correspondingly more circumspect. The Emperor, they said, would be deified after his death, as Hercules, Romulus and others had been, for his services to mankind.

All this adulation is alien to our modern way of feeling, though it was much less so to that of the sixteenth to eighteenth centuries, from 'Gloriana' to the 'Roi Soleil', when such rhetoric was not expected to be taken literally. We must exercise historical imagination. If the proem to Book 3 can be accepted as an eagle-flight of Pindaric fancy, that of Book 1 can be accepted as an extravagance of Alexandrian-style baroque. Both are masterly, and exhilarating in their way.

With the social policy of Augustanism, which writers such as Virgil and Horace may have done much to create on their own initiative, the *Georgics* is sincerely in tune, and not only as regards the spiritual unification of Italy. The respect shown for rustic piety as well as national religion, the ideal of the chaste family with children clinging to their parents' necks, the commendation of Italian peoples, of which the Sabines were typical, for their simplicity and hardiness, and of the pacifying prowess of Roman arms abroad, combined with a deep craving for peace at home – all this was in line. To some extent the bees' commonwealth in Book 4 may be meant as an exemplar – their single-minded, unselfish co-operation, their industry, their devotion to their leader. But the comparison must not be pressed too far: their communality of habitation and offspring, for instance, excluded the Augustan focus on home and family life (see pp. 120–21).

RELIGION AND PHILOSOPHY

We saw that in his twenties Virgil was enjoying at Naples the quietism of Siro's Epicurean garden. To this quietism the *Bucolics*, with their atmosphere of pastoral leisure and their dreams of a Golden Age paradise, were attuned. It persists in the very different context of the *Georgics* to the extent that the poet disclaims worldly ambitions: he wants to be left to love unglamorously the rivers and woods (2.485), to enjoy 'the studies of inglorious ease' (4.564). There are also moments when we hear the rationalistic tones of Lucretius, for instance in his preference for a biochemical to a supernatural explanation of how rooks presage the weather (1.415 –23). But in general there has been a change, not, one may think, because he has now entered the circle of Maecenas and come near to the political centre, but because previously he had been carried away by a trend, and particularly by the impassioned poetry of Lucretius, into a view of the universe that did not really reflect his own nature. He was well aware of the ultimate contrast between his mentality and that of Lucretius. Using phrases reminiscent of him in a famous passage from his eulogy of country life at the end of Book 2 he wrote (475–86; 490–94):

> For my own part my chiefest prayer would be:
> May the sweet Muses whose acolyte I am,
> Smitten with boundless love, accept my service,
> Teach me to know the paths of the stars in heaven,
> The eclipses of the sun and the moon's travails,
> The cause of earthquakes, what it is that forces
> Deep seas to swell and burst their barriers
> And then sink back again, why winter suns
> Hasten so fast to plunge themselves in the ocean
> Or what it is that slows the lingering nights.
> But if some chill in the blood about the heart
> Bars me from mastering these sides of nature,
> Then will I pray that I may find fulfilment
> In the country and the streams that water valleys,
> Love rivers and woods, unglamorous . . .
> Blessèd is he whose mind had power to probe
> The causes of things and trample underfoot
> All terrors and inexorable fate
> And the clamour of devouring Acheron;
> But happy too is he who knows the gods
> Of the countryside . . .

He is said to have hoped to devote his life, after he had finished his epic, to philosophy; but one may doubt whether much would have come of it. He was a feeler rather than a thinker. His genius was for ordering his insights into great works of poetic art.

Varro, in his lost work on *Religious Antiquities*, had formulated traditional Roman attitudes to religion. It was of three kinds: mythological (that of the poets); natural (that of the philosophers); and civic (that of the statesmen). At the beginning of his *De Re Rustica* he invokes twelve gods (a canonical number, even if the individuals varied), not the twelve urban ones, he adds, whose statues might be seen round the Forum, male and female in pairs, but the special patron gods of husbandmen. The somewhat different twelve invoked by Virgil in the prologue to his poem are not only Olympians such as Neptune (Poseidon) and Minerva (Athena), Liber (Bacchus) and Ceres (Demeter), but Pan, Triptolemus, Aristaeus and the Italian Silvanus, and more shadowy spirits of the woods, Fauns (like the Greek Satyrs) and Dryad nymphs. These are likewise 'country gods' such as he counts himself fortunate to know, and they make their appearance here and there throughout the poem. They belong to the category of 'the religion of the poets', ultimately Greek.

But Jupiter in the poem, except in so far as he is the sky god, belongs to 'the religion of the philosophers'. He appears first in Book 1 at line 121 as 'the Father himself'. He is Providence, the Zeus of the Stoics, who has ordained that man should have difficulties to overcome so as to sharpen his wits and keep him from degenerating into sloth. This is by contrast with the dispensation of his father Saturn (Kronos), the god of the Golden Age paradise whom he supplanted. Jupiter introduced 'hard primitivism' instead of 'soft primitivism'.[1] His world is not that of the *Bucolics* or of the Epicureans. Hesiod had explained man's troubles, symbolized by his hiding of fire, as a punishment for Prometheus' offence (*Works and Days* 42–50). Lucretius had adduced the faults in creation and the troubles they cause as evidence that the universe could not have been divinely created (5.195–221). Virgil echoes

1. For the terms see A. O. Lovejoy and G. Boas, *Primitivism and Related Ideas in Antiquity* (1935), pp. 10–11.

these passages as to the reality of the troubles, but he feels a need to 'justify the ways of God to men'. For this purpose he espouses an old Greek idea, found, for instance, in the proem to Aratus' *Phaenomena* and developed by the Stoics: it is from benevolence that God has prescribed toil for man, as a trainer prescribes painful exercises for athletes. Another idea, that there is a compensation for hard work in the variety of life due to technical progress, can be felt in lines 129–45 (see pp. 35–8). To St Thomas Aquinas the supreme beauty (*summus decor*) of the universe was the order by which things are dissimilar.

The idea of divine providence occurs elsewhere in the poem. It is the gods' bounty that has assigned to mortals two temperate zones of the earth in which to live (1.238); it is 'the Father himself' who has given them signs to presage the weather (1.353). The wonderful order of the bees' commonwealth is a special reward from Jupiter (4.149). The contemplation of this order leads to another passage in which Platonic-Stoic ideas emerge (4.219–27):

> Led by these signs and by these instances
> Some have affirmed that bees possess a share
> Of the divine mind and drink ethereal draughts;
> For God, they say, pervades the whole creation,
> Lands and the sea's expanse and the depths of sky.
> Thence flocks and herds and men and all the beasts
> Of the wild derive, each in his hour of birth,
> The subtle breath of life; and surely thither
> All things at last return, dissolved, restored.
> There is no room for death: alive they fly
> To join the stars and mount aloft to Heaven.

Here Virgil is professing only to retail the ideas of others; but he does so with evident sympathy, and the fact that a few years later, in the *Aeneid* (6.724–32), he made similar views the basis of Anchises' exposition of the nature of the universe to his son Aeneas confirms that sympathy. The passage is, in a sense, the culmination of one of the most pervasive features of the poem: Virgil's sympathy with all nature, animate and inanimate (see pp. 42–4).

It was widely held among educated Romans that it was of the greatest importance to maintain the religious traditions of the community, even after, for them, Greek rationalism had shaken or demolished literal belief in the gods. This was 'the religion of the statesmen', regarded less as 'the opium of the people' than as something which bound together citizens of every degree, embodying Roman feeling somewhat as the Orthodox Church embodies Hellenic feeling in modern Greece. There were atheists, of course, and men like the Epicureans who believed that the gods existed but that they influenced mortals only by being an example of detached serenity for them to contemplate and emulate; but most were careful not to proclaim their scepticism beyond the reading public.

At the climax of *Georgics* I (498) Virgil appeals to the gods of Rome specifically, native gods, to allow 'this young man' (Caesar) to save the ruined state. 'The statesmen's religion' is only prominent in the poem, apart from two descriptions of rustic festivals, in this and the other passages that treat of Caesar as a candidate for deification. The idea of invoking him as an extra, special deity after a canonical twelve had precedents in Greece, with Philip and Alexander; but no man previously had been so honoured at Rome (see p. 26). The idea of worshipping someone's *genius*, which was something like his personality but conceived of as an attendant spirit or guardian angel, was not incomprehensible to Roman feeling. But Virgil and Horace had close contact with Caesar as a man, and however much they may have been under the spell of his charismatic personality, it is not necessary to suppose that they literally believed him to be a god on earth, or even that he would become a god after death.

These religious elements, poetic, philosophical or political, should not be taken as evidence of belief in our sense of the word (even Lucretius began by invoking Venus); they are rather symbols of numinous feelings about various aspects of life and the universe. Yet in particular cases a god may have been real even to an educated person, as a patron saint might be to some Catholic today. Augustus, for instance, clearly had a special devotion to Apollo and all that he stood for – order, beauty, civilization. Virgil may have felt sometimes that there was indeed a power working in the universe for an order that was ultimately providential, personified as 'the Father himself'.

But it is impossible to make the *Georgics* yield a consistent view of the nature of things. If Jupiter is a providential father, why is everything fated to degenerate (1.199)? If he has purposely made things hard in order to sharpen the wits and train the character of men, how can it be said that the earth freely lavishes on the farmer an easy livelihood and that the fields willingly produce crops of their own accord (2.460; 500)? The poem, like human life, embodies a variety of moods; but the moods, unlike those of life, are organized into a controlled structure. It is the overall impression that counts.

AGRICULTURAL LORE

Many readers have been struck by the amount of what is now recognized as sound advice on agriculture that is to be found in the *Georgics*. We must begin by inquiring how much is likely to be first-hand. There was a large body of Greek prose-writing on the subject, some of it by eminent authorities. Varro (1.8–9) names more than fifty such writers whose works were available for consultation. Much of their work has now been lost; but some survives, such as treatises on animals by Aristotle and on plants by his pupil and successor Theophrastus, and we can see that Virgil consulted these. In Latin the extant works of Cato and Varro have been mentioned; but those of others have been lost, including the most important by far, the translation of those of Mago the Carthaginian made by order of the Senate. Most of Virgil's precepts can be found in extant writers, whose accounts are much fuller. He cannot win: for if he alone of extant writers says something right, he may well have been drawing on a lost predecessor; whereas if he says something wrong, he either must have misinterpreted someone or at least cannot be drawing on personal experience. Let us take two examples. Virgil warns us (3.388) that if a ram has so much as a black tongue it may beget blotchy lambs. This, though it used to be dismissed as a myth, has been independently confirmed in the case of Turkish Karakul sheep (1936) and Swedish Gotland sheep (1963);[1] but Virgil cannot be given the credit, since a similar warning is given by Aristotle and Varro. On the other hand when he claims (2.67–71) that walnut can be grafted on to arbutus, apple on to plane, beech on to chestnut, pear

1. See L. P. Wilkinson, *The Georgics of Virgil*, p. 257 n.

on to ash and oak on to elm, he is so wildly wrong that it is hard to conceive that he had much experience of arboriculture. Yet although there is little evidence that he was ever a practical farmer, there are touches throughout the poem which suggest that he was a keen observer of nature and of what is done on farms.

Further general discussion and information on this subject will be found in the introductions to the several Books and, as to details, in the notes.

THE POEM

The basic framework of the poem is as follows:

Book 1: Field Crops

1–42	Proem to the whole work: invocation to country gods and Caesar.
43–203	Work, especially on field crops.
204–350	The farmer's calendar.
351–463	Weather-signs, leading into
463–514	Portents of Rome's disasters and prayer for salvation.

Book 2: Trees

1–8, 39–46	Invocations to Bacchus and to Maecenas.
9–38, 47–258	Variety, especially as regards trees (136–76: eulogy of Italy).
259–457	Care of trees, especially vines.
458–540	Eulogy of country life.
451–2	Epilogue.

Book 3: Animals

1–48	Proem, to Maecenas. The poet and Caesar.
49–283	Part I: large animals; horses and cattle (209–83: sex).
284–92	Proem to Part II.
295–473	Part II: small animals; sheep and goats.
475–566	The Noric animal plague.

Book 4: Bees

The work falls into two pairs of Books, concerning vegetable and animal husbandry respectively. Each pair has an extensive 'external' proem, relating the poem to the great world, whereas Books 2 and 4 have only a short 'internal' proem. The proem to Book 1 introduces the whole poem, and Book 4 concludes with an epilogue to the whole poem. In 1 and 3 the tone tends to be sombre; toil is emphasized, and each culminates in a dramatic description of catastrophe. 2 and 4 are more cheerful (the Aristaeus episode apart), and the tone is lighter. But the architecture of the poem is much more subtly integrated than any exposure of the bare framework can suggest.[1]

Suetonius (22) records a tradition that Virgil, in composing the *Georgics*, used to dictate every day lines composed in the early morning and then spend the rest of the day in reducing them to a very small number, aptly remarking that he was like a she-bear gradually licking her cubs into shape. This is unlikely to be quite accurate. Thus a poet in whom the sense is, in Milton's phrase, 'variously drawn out from line to line' is unlikely to have composed with the line as his unit. But he may have produced spontaneously a number of metrical phrases and then welded them selectively into continuous sentences and periods. If indeed he spent seven years on the poem, the story is not surprising: quite apart from studying and comparing his sources, he must have devoted much time both to organization and to expressive and harmonious verbal art, not to mention revision.

1. An outline of the contents is given in the introduction to each Book. The vexed question of the status in the textual tradition of the Aristaeus episode with that of Orpheus inset is discussed in the introduction to Book 4.

The poem is diversified by 'set pieces'. Most of these can be certainly or plausibly dated on internal evidence as having been among the latest to be composed, or at least completed, though the first part of the finale of Book I suggests rather the agonies of the mid-thirties. But it would be quite wrong to separate the poem into watertight compartments, didactic and ornamental. It is a veritable Proteus: if you try to tie it down to a particular subject, or even genre, it slips through your fingers.

If one were obliged however to assign the *Georgics* to some particular genre, ruling out 'didactic' as one should and taking into account the poem as a whole and the good that can be derived from reading it, the answer must surely be 'descriptive'. So Michael Grant decided in his *Roman Literature* (1954). It must rank in that case as the first such poem in Western literature known to us. Jacques Perret also calls it 'one of the few successful descriptive poems that man can find in his age-old archives' (*Virgile*, 1959, p. 79). Previous poets had introduced short descriptive passages, vividly realized, as relief. Hesiod's vignettes of summer and winter have already been mentioned (p. 17). Theocritus had made his Seventh Idyll culminate in a luscious description of harvest-time. Greek rhetoricians had given such passages the name of *ekphrasis*, and they were so seductive that orators had to be warned against dragging them in irrelevantly. Horace gives poets a similar warning at the beginning of his *Ars Poetica*. But Virgil could learn from Lucretius in particular the delight that can be given by vivid imagery and accumulated detail that generate a landscape or scene of activity. The pleasure we can derive from it is akin to that we derive from landscape or genre painting. The total effect is a panorama of rural life, a supremely artistic documentary. The young Addison, in his anonymous essay prefixed to Dryden's translation of the *Georgics*, wrote perceptively: 'This kind of poetry I am now speaking of addresses itself wholly to the imagination . . . It raises in our minds a pleasing variety of scenes and landskips whilst it teaches us, and makes the dryest of its precepts look like a description.' And again: 'We find our imaginations more affected by his descriptions than they would have been by the very sight of what he describes.'

When Wordsworth revised his poems it was, as his manuscripts show, in order to make his phrasing correspond more accurately and vividly to his ideas. We may imagine that Virgil was to a large extent similarly occupied on those afternoons Suetonius spoke of. This 'expressiveness', that is, the accommodation of sounds and rhythms to sense, was something by which he evidently set great store, but it can only be illustrated from the Latin. In this he resembled Tennyson in particular among English poets. To take a rather obvious example: in Tennyson's poem *The Brook* the brook's reply is a study in such virtuosity:

> I chatter over stony ways
>   In little sharps and trebles.
> I bubble into eddying bays.
>   I babble on the pebbles . . .

When Virgil came to describe a farmer making a runnel (1.108) he took his cue from a very expressive simile in Homer (*Iliad* 21.257 ff.) and produced sounds that anticipate Tennyson's:

>   cum exustus ager morientibus aestuat herbis,
> ecce supercilio clivosi tramitis undam
> elicit; illa cadens raucum per levia murmur
> saxa ciet scatebrisque arentia temperat arva.

> . . . Who, when exhausted
> The earth swelters with dying verdure, look,
> Down from the brow of a sloping pathway tempts
> A trickle that murmurs purling over the pebbles
> To cool the parched-up ground? . . .

There are large portions of Virgil's text in which this descriptive quality is uppermost. For instance, the lines devoted to the weather-signs, more than a hundred (1.351–462), though ostensibly utilitarian and also adduced as evidence of divine providence for men, are so vividly presented that their appeal is to our appreciation of their kaleidoscopic imagery.

'Kaleidoscopic' is the word. It may seem odd to stress variety as a cardinal element in the success of a poem, but the importance of variation (*poikilia*) had been recognized by Greek critics, and Servius (3.195) uses it to justify Virgil's insertion of a passage about cattle in the context of flocks. Erich Burck was surely right in diagnosing enthusiasm for this as the distinguishing feature of the first main part of Book 2 – variety in methods of propagating trees, of trees themselves, of vintages, of lands; and it is indeed a feature

of the whole poem. Lucretius (5.1448–57) had praised the variety
that had been introduced into human life by gradual progress due
to man's experience, experiment and ingenuity: 'Shipping and
agriculture, walls, laws, weapons, dress and so forth, the rewards
and luxuries of life as a whole, songs and pictures and polished
sculptures intricately wrought.' The same enthusiasm can be felt,
despite the relentless labour involved, in Virgil's description of
progress under Jupiter's dispensation (1.136–44):

>   . . . Then first upon their backs
> Rivers felt boats of hollowed alder, then
> Mariners grouped the stars and gave them names,
> Pleiads and Hyads and the radiant Bear,
> Lycaon's daughter. Now was found the way
> To snare wild beasts with nets and birds with lime
> And cordon off wide coverts with rings of hounds.
> One lashes a broad river with a cast-net
> Probing the depths, another drags through the sea
> His dripping trawl. Next hardened iron came
> And the creaking saw-blade (for the earliest men
> Split wood with wedges), and last the various arts.

Lucretius in a previous passage (5.1370–78) described the variety
of landscapes that progress in agriculture had produced:

And day by day they forced the woods to recede up the mountains and give
up the land below to cultivation, so that on hillsides and plains they might
have meadows, ponds, streams, crops and glad vineyards and let a belt of
grey olive trees run between to make a clear division, stretching over
mounds and hollows and level ground, even as now you see the whole
patterned with the charm of variety (*vario distincta lepore*), where men
beautify it by planting fruit-trees here and there and keep it hedged around
with fertile shrubs.

A similar delight in variety keeps breaking out in the *Georgics*,
variety both in activity and spectacle, as at 2.516–22:

>   Never a pause!
> The seasons teem with fruits, the young of flocks,
> Or sheaves of Ceres' corn; they load the furrows
> And burst the barns with produce. Then, come winter,
> The olive-press is busy; sleek with acorns
> The pigs come home; the arbutes in the woods
> Give berries; autumn sheds its varied windfalls;
> And high on sunny terraces of rock
> The mellow vintage ripens.

The inner eye ranges from image to image as Virgil details the tasks
that can occupy a farmer in the winter (1.261–74):

> Ploughmen beat sharp the blunted ploughshare point;
> Troughs can be scooped from tree-trunks, flocks be branded
> And heaps of corn be labelled. Some will sharpen
> Two-pronged supports and stakes, others prepare
> Amerian withes to tie the trailing vine.
> Now weave the pliant basket of bramble-shoots,
> Now roast your grain, now grind it on your millstone.
> Even on holy days the laws of gods
> And men permit some tasks: no scruple ever
> Forbade to clear out runnels, make a fence
> For crops, set traps for birds, burn briar-thickets,
> Or dip the bleating flock in a stream for health.
> Often the driver of a dawdling donkey
> Will load its flanks with oil or low-grade fruit
> On a holy day, and bring back home from town
> A chiselled millstone or a lump of pitch.

Gerard Manley Hopkins' poem *Pied Beauty* expresses a delight like
that of Lucretius and Virgil in the variety of human activity and the
spectacle it has produced, attributing it, as Virgil does, to 'Pater
ipse':

> Landscape plotted and pieced – fold, fallow and plough;
>> And all trades, their gear and tackle and trim.
> All things counter, original, spare, strange;
>> Whatever is fickle, freckled (who knows how?)
>>> With swift, slow; sweet, sour; adazzle, dim;
> He fathers-forth whose beauty is past change:
>> Praise him.

'Swift, slow; sweet, sour; adazzle, dim': these contrasts are
analogous to *chiaroscuro* in painting. Contrasts are a feature of the
Georgics, a fact well brought out in Klingner's running commentary. G. Ramain first drew attention to the visual contrast between
the shadow-seeking viper and adder and the dazzling Calabrian
snake that rages abroad and towers towards the sun (3.414–39);
between the cranes coming down from the upper air and the heifer
looking up at the sky to sniff the breezes, the flitting swallow and
the frogs down in the mud, the tiny ant pursuing its narrow path
and the huge, overarching rainbow (1.374–89). After the dark and
devastating storm at 1.311–34 the sun comes out for the rustic

spring festival. The whole eulogy of country life at the end of Book 2 is built up of contrasts, 'if not . . . yet . . .' – between country simplicity and urban extravagance, urban restlessness and country tranquillity, scientific understanding and simple faith, country peace and world politics, political crime and country innocence, fratricidal war and family concord, the old dispensation of Saturn and the new dispensation of Jupiter. In the eulogy of Italy (2.136 –76) the exotic East is contrasted with the golden mean of the West. An idyllic picture of early summer in the homeland (3.332 –8) is followed by vivid vignettes of contrasting extremes, the life of the Libyan shepherd in the torrid South and of the Scythian hunter in the frozen North. At 3.49–94 the shambling, serviceable cow contrasts with the mettlesome thoroughbred racehorse.

Such contrasts were obviously contrived on purpose. Analogous ones have been observed in the arrangement of subjects in contemporary wall-paintings. Virgil also likes to couple Greek names his reader would know from literature with Italian ones he might know from experience. It is the same with style: a passage of high poetry such as the eulogy of Italy is followed abruptly with one of down-to-earth, almost prosaic, agricultural instruction. He does not shrink from ugliness when it is appropriate, but he may offset it with relief: after the repellent description of how to kill a calf for the creation of new bees he introduces a breath of fresh air to banish a nasty smell (4.305–7):

> All this occurs in the season when the Zephyrs
> First ruffle the waves, before the fields begin
> To redden with spring colours, and before
> The chattering swallow hangs her nest from the rafters.

Several critics have likened the *Georgics* to a musical composition. Klingner calls it 'a composition in many tones in which a number of themes develop, come to the fore, die away and make place for new ones.' The military metaphor may serve as an instance, the idea of man as waging a continual war with the degenerative forces of nature: he 'disciplines the acres he commands' (1.99). After throwing the seed he grapples with the land at close quarters (1.104–5). His implements are weapons (1.160). The theme emerges more fully at 2.279–83, where the method of planting vines on a hillside is compared with the deploying of a legion in regularly spaced ranks and files before a battle. It is heard again at 2.369: 'then exercise hard discipline and curb the straggling branches.' The nomad African herdsman, moving with all his gear strung around him, is compared at 3.346–8 with a keen Roman legionary accomplishing a forced march under his country's arms with their cruel load, to encamp and fall in for battle before his enemy is aware. And finally we have the full-scale battle of the bees, conceived in human terms, at 4.67–85.

Other recurrent themes may be characterized, for instance, as Hard Work, Foreign Lands, Seafaring, Religion, Providence, Prognostics, Olympic Games. As in some other works of literature that have didactic treatises behind them, such as Cicero's *De Oratore* and Horace's *Ars Poetica*, the handbook boundaries between topics are cunningly bridged over (except for the break between large and small animals in Book 3, marked by a fresh proem). Thus the long passage on weather-signs (1.356–468) is heralded by admonitions to watch the stars (204–30; 335–7), their attribution to Providence, by 231–9 (*idcirco; munere divum*). There are also balances of theme. Thus the simile of the runaway boat at the end of the first part of Book 1 (201–3) is balanced by that of the runaway chariot at the end of the second (512–4). The eulogy of Italy in the middle of Book 2 is balanced by the eulogy of country life at the end of it. The grim picture in the middle of Book 3 of the havoc that can be caused by sex is balanced by the one at the end of it of the havoc that can be caused by plague. In Book 3 Virgil varies the order of the material he found in Varro so as to make horses and cattle, sheep and goats alternate, for the sake of variety and to make the larger animals precede the smaller so that the former may return with greater effect in the grand finale of the Plague. The theme of Death, given out at 66–8, recurs at 258–68 (Leander and Glaucus) and 368 (the trapped beasts in Scythia), and swells to a veritable Triumph of Death in the Plague.

But the most remarkable contributor to the variety of the poem is its climax, the Aristaeus episode, occupying the latter half of Book 4 and here assumed to be part of the original text (see p. 122). By contrast with the rest it is narrative. Its form is that of an 'epyllion', the short kind of epic popular in the Alexandrianizing 'modernistic' ambience in which Virgil grew up. A feature of this was that the story had another story inset which is somehow, directly or obliquely, relevant to it, if only by way of contrast. The framework of 171 lines, the Aristaeus story, is based on ideas from Homer and is told in Homeric style, objectively, with scenery and action vividly described in detail. The inset, the Orpheus story, is quite different, as Otis ably demonstrated. It is told subjectively. It is full of pathos. We feel that Virgil himself, not the grotesque Proteus, is speaking. In Alexandrian fashion it is elliptical and asymmetrical. Highly important events, Eurydice's death and the conditional relenting of Dis and Proserpine, are referred to only retrospectively and obliquely: everything is concentrated on the fatal moment when Orpheus looked back (*respexit*). And then there is the supreme contrast of the poem, between the vast mountain landscape and the lonely mourner.

What can have led Virgil to give his poem such a surprising conclusion, which makes it less possible than ever to categorize by genre? It is natural that he should have wished not to omit anything so dramatic as the apparent miracle of *Bugonia*, which Varro had placed in the forefront of his account (3.16.4), natural indeed that he should transfer it to the end as climax. To anyone in the Alexandrian tradition it was natural that any elaboration should take the form of an *aition*, a myth about the origin of a custom. And the most natural figure about whom to weave such a myth (for to the best of our knowledge he invented it) was Aristaeus, son of the healer Apollo, pupil of the healer Chiron, who, taught by the Nymphs, became the patron of beekeepers. It was a personal loss (of his son Actaeon) that was said to have brought Aristaeus as a wanderer to the isle of Ceos, where he redeemed the people from pestilence by initiating them into novel sacrifices. Faced with inventing a myth, Virgil did what most Roman poets would do: he had recourse to Greek literature. Homer provided him with the idea of a hero (Achilles) appealing when stricken by loss (of Briseis, *Iliad* 1.357 ff., and of Patroclus, *Iliad* 18.35 ff.) to a divine mother who lived beneath the waters (Thetis), and also of a hero (Menelaus) seeking oracular information from Proteus (*Odyssey* 4.351 ff.).

It was natural also for someone inventing an epyllion to have an inset story, but Virgil, so far as we know, was the first to connect Orpheus with Aristaeus, by making the traditional death of Orpheus' wife Eurydice by a snakebite the result of amorous pursuit of her by Aristaeus, though there was a tradition that Orpheus after his death was an angry daemon who had to be appeased by proper sacrifices. Also, the story of the second loss of Eurydice caused by Orpheus' disobedience in looking back at her is unknown in any pre-Virgilian version. Nor did the plot require that Proteus should dwell at such length on the story of Orpheus – only that his anger and that of the Nymphs with Aristaeus should be revealed as the cause of the death of the bees. The conclusion of the Aristaeus story (530–58) is so short as to be perfunctory: Virgil has already pre-empted it by describing *Bugonia* in its contemporary form at 295–314. What echoes in the reader's mind is not Aristaeus' joy at the replacement of his bees but Orpheus' thrice-repeated cry in death of 'Eurydice'. It is his tragic disobedience and his inconsolable grief that Virgil throws into relief. Why?

Scholars are still discussing the question: how can the Aristaeus story, and that of Orpheus in particular, be more than superficially relevant to the poem as a whole? Klingner, for instance (*Virgils Georgica*, pp. 234 ff.) saw a connection in lines 219–27, the passage that reports the opinion of some that bees share in the divine spirit that pervades the universe. The life of the individual is fraught with pain, tragedy and death; but existence is also the all-pervading and joyfully stirring spirit of life, so that, universally speaking, 'there is no room for death.' Disease and death for man and beast, represented in Book 3 as without redemption, are redeemed and absorbed into a higher divine order. As for the relevance of Orpheus, Virgil has interwoven two contrasting stories (as Catullus in his Peleus and Thetis epyllion interwove with their happy marriage the desertion of Ariadne by Theseus), two representations of life and death: of life newly granted and ever again to be rewon; and life lost, sought with passionate love, almost snatched from death, and then for ever sinking back into the underworld.

This interpretation, typifying those that seek relevance through large abstractions, lays more stress on the replacement of the bees than Virgil seems to do. Those who find it too abstract and high-flown may prefer, for instance, an approach such as that of Jasper Griffin. He rightly insists that the effective emphasis is on the Orpheus story, for which Aristaeus and *Bugonia* provide a pretext. The bees' kingdom represents the old Roman ideal of an impersonal and collective state, which Augustus was to some extent to revive. Pointedly, their close connection in Greek tradition with song and poetry is suppressed: these are represented by Orpheus, who stands for the life of the individual, associated in particular with the bitter-sweet pains and pleasures of love. One side of Virgil's nature could not be satisfied with the impersonal idea of the state. He is here moving towards the Aeneid, 'a poem of loss, defeat and pathos as much as it is of triumphant destiny.' The discourse of Anchises in *Aeneid* 6 juxtaposes the two aspects and leaves them unresolved. In a more light-hearted way the epilogue to the *Georgics* had done the same. Augustus had to emphasize law and order: the finale of *Georgics* 1 makes that clear. But Virgil never underestimated the cost in human terms (see p. 25). Whatever its relevance to the rest of the poem, the Aristaeus epyllion, and particularly the Orpheus passage, remains one of the most beautiful and moving achievements of Latin literature.

Turning to other features of the *Georgics*, there is the tendency to humanize everything: where Aratus remarks objectively that on a misty night snuff gathers on the nozzle of a lamp (976), Virgil says (1.390), 'Even girls spinning their nightly stint of wool indoors, are made aware . . .' The ubiquitous attribution of human feeling to nature, both animate and inanimate, seems to come naturally to him. Fields have characters (*ingenia*): they can be churlish or torpid; they have to be disciplined and exercised; but they can also be helped and gladdened, and their crops can lift up their spirits. Rivers feel boats on their backs; the moon blushes and the sun feels pity and hides his head. Trees and shrubs in Book 2 are particularly sentient. They can be schooled to put off their wild spirit and collaborate in learning arts; but they must be kept up to the mark, otherwise they will forget. They array themselves in blossom and fruit. To produce them, shoots are torn from their mother's tender side. They recognize the mother soil from which they came. Young vines must be inured gradually to submit to the pruning-knife. Even a wine catalogue is animated by an assumption of rivalry between lordly vintages, whose feelings can also be hurt. The smallest of animals, too, are somehow human: the fieldmouse establishes his granaries under the floor, and the ant worries about providing for her old age. A deep sympathy informs the simile, inspired by Homer, of the nightingale lamenting all night in a poplar-tree for her hapless young whom a heartless ploughman has spied and dragged from her nest (4.511–15). Virgil makes us share in the chattering joy of the rooks revisiting their young after a storm. Elsewhere they are like legionaries forming a column of route to evacuate their mess-ground. His farmer is a realist: production must have priority. But Virgil spares a thought for the rooks evicted from their ancestral homes by the woodcutter (2.207–11). You must resist the temptation to leave honey for the bees over winter, however grieved they are at its destruction, for it would harbour pests. If your hive shows signs of swarming, you must tear off the leaders' wings. The inferior of two leaders must be summarily killed.

Bees, of course, invite anthropomorphic treatment, and Virgil exploits this to the full. Otherwise, the larger the animal, the greater the sympathy. But again you must be realistic. If a sheep has scab, you must nerve yourself to lance the ulcer; if it has a contagious disease, you must kill it. You may have to be ruthless even with the largest animals: even your prize stallion, when his potency begins to fail, must be shut up without remorse. It is natural that Virgil should have had a special feeling for the ox, who was so close a fellow-worker with man in the operation of ploughing. In the poignant description at 3.515–30 of the ox that falls dead of the plague while still in harness he imagines the things he must have enjoyed in life – shade in deep woods, clear running streams and rest in grassy meadows, innocent pleasures between useful labours that deserved a better reward. He imagines too the grief of his bereaved yokemate, inspired here by Lucretius. In the only passage where he mentions the milking of cows (3.176–8) he appeals to the herdsman not to make the beasts, after calving, fill his pail as farmers usually do, dedicated to squeezing out the last drop of profit, but to let them spend it on their own 'cherished offspring', the phrase he uses elsewhere of children clinging to their returning father's neck. The lovely heifer at 3.219–41 for whom two lovesick bulls are rivals is thoroughly human and knows what she is doing with her 'fetching wiles'. She does not let them concentrate on feeding, but constrains them to fight for her. The defeated bull behaves like a man: sadly he goes into exile from his ancestral domain and husbands his strength to return and 'advance his standards to battle'. The racehorse shares his owner's desire to win. In selecting a stallion for breeding you must look for 'the grief of each in losing, his pride in victory'; 'their thirst for praise, their will to win' (3.100–112). In speaking of breeding horses Virgil uses ordinary human terms, 'father', 'mother', 'husband', and even terms that had religious connotations for the Romans, 'Lucina' (goddess of childbirth) and 'weddings'. And when he comes to the great power of sexual lust he makes no distinctions – *amor omnibus idem* (242–4): in his instances he passes straight from the Sabine boar to the youth who was fatally driven by lust to attempt to swim the Hellespont by night in a storm (258–63).

In dealing with small animals Virgil also shows a gentle sense of humour, a touch of irony or parody, which is particularly evident in the first hundred lines of Book 4, where mock-epic language is sometimes used of the bees. When introducing sheep and goats, on the other hand, he remarks 'how great a task it is . . . to invest such humble things with dignity' (3.290). In choosing to treat everyday matters of farming in heroic hexameters he was endowing them with dignity from the start. But he has various other methods. It is hard for us, even if we are familiar with classical history, geography and mythology, to recapture the pleasure that allusions to them must have given to a Roman proud of his new Greek education. Our nearest parallel, perhaps, is the pleasure that Milton's allusions to the classics and the Bible must have given to seventeenth-century readers. Why is the spider at 4.246 gratuitously called 'Minerva's hate'? Because its ancestress was the girl Arachne, turned into a spider for challenging the goddess to a spinning match (Ovid tells the story at the beginning of *Metamorphoses* 6). It is only a fleeting reference, of no apparent significance beyond the pleasure of recognition – ultimately one of self-congratulation. (Such references have occasionally been omitted in the translation if they get in the way.) After detailing the points of a good war-horse Virgil instances the horses of gods and heroes, Pollux, Mars and Achilles, and the epic dignity imparted is appropriate and appreciable. But he concludes with Saturn hastily transforming himself into a stallion when caught by his wife with a girl (3.89–94). I am less sure than a recent critic that magnificence would have been the impression made by this on the contemporaries of Ovid. Glamorous and resounding legendary names however probably appealed to Virgil's as to Milton's readers:

> Phillyrides Chiron Amathaoniusque Melampus.
> Lancelot and Pelleas and Pellenore.

Geographical names were also sometimes used simply, it would seem, as ornament. An Italian farmer would not really have to fear being waylaid by Iberian bandits; nor would a Libyan shepherd be likely to have a Cretan quiver, let alone a dog from Amyclae, near Sparta.

Sometimes mythology is used in a more integral way. Varro tells us that honey should be gathered three times a year, first when the Pleiads are rising. Virgil (reducing the number; 4.231–5) elaborates:

> Twice in the year men gather the honey harvest:
> First when Taÿgetê the Pleiad shows
> Her comely face to the world and with her foot
> Has spurned the streams of Ocean, and again
> When the same star, fleeing the rainy Sign
> Of the Fish, more sadly hastens down the sky
> Into the wintry waves.

Why is this moving? Why 'more sadly'? Surely because Taÿgetê is a reminder of the fate of us all. The imagery suggests the confident rise of man in his youthful beauty and the tearful sadness of his decline into chilly death. It is touches like this that transform precept into poetry. In dealing with the stars in particular Virgil recaptures the imagination of the primitive sailors who saw them as suggestive of human and animal forms, as at 1.217–18:

> When with his gilded horns the dazzling Bull
> Opens the year, and the Dog backs down before him.

Virgil also avoids monotony by ringing the changes on syntactical constructions, rhetorical figures and enjambement of verse. After the impetuosity of the proem he keeps his sentences fairly short unless there is reason to do otherwise: they should be comfortable to recite. He has also learnt from his study of rhetoric that a longer clause may effectively sum up a series of shorter ones – often a single, self-contained verse. He will hold up the operative word, generally a verb, to fall decisively at the beginning of a line. The shape of his sentences and his verses sometimes in itself contributes to the expressiveness, the representation of the sense by the form which matters so much for the descriptive quality of the poem (see p. 35).

As to diction, it is hard to generalize. Some passages are obviously epic, some obviously down-to-earth. Virgil does not hesitate, for instance, to name dung (*fimus*). But he does not seem to descend to plebeianism, and slang would be out of place in a translation. Our means of diagnosing the tone of Latin words are limited. In general Virgil seems to observe the sovereign classical principle of 'propriety'.

But all the various features and qualities mentioned in this introduction would not, even taken together, have sufficed to raise the *Georgics* to the heights ('the best poem of the best poet' was Dryden's perhaps extravagant judgement), were it not for Virgil's sensitive mastery of his vehicle and of the Latin language. This the Latinless reader must be asked to take on trust, with the hope that even in English something of the poem's unique quality may shine through – though English can hardly be expected, for instance, to cope with the sonorous monumentality of a line such as

Laomedontēae luimŭs periuria Troiae.

DOWN THE AGES

In antiquity the *Georgics* shared with Virgil's other works in his fame as a poet. It was as poetry that it was read by Seneca, for instance, in the first century A.D. As a guide to agriculture, if Virgil was taken too seriously by Columella, he was freely criticized by the elder Pliny. Descriptive poetry also graduated to a genre, well exemplified by Ausonius' poem on the river Moselle (*c.* 400 A.D.).

In the millennium 400–1400 Virgil remained the supreme poet for those who still read, but there is much less evidence for the reading of the *Georgics* than of the *Bucolics* and *Aeneid*. It probably gave Walafrid Strabo of Reichenau on Lake Constance in the early ninth century the idea for his *Hortulus*, a poem in quite accomplished Latin hexameters on the uses of various plants. It certainly had more direct influence on a poem of the same period by another German monk, Wandalbert of Prüm, in equally accomplished hexameters, on the twelve months, describing rural life in mid-Rhineland; for there are frequent verbal reminiscences. But these two poems are exceptional. There is more evidence in the Middle Ages for 'spiritual Georgics', works in which the husbandry is allegorical for the tending of the Christian soul.

In the Renaissance however the *Georgics* is freely cited, from Petrarch onwards. Politian composed his *Rusticus* (1483) in 570 Latin hexameters for recitation as a prologue to his lectures on Hesiod and the *Georgics*. In the next century the vernacular tended to take over, with poems in Italian – Giovanni Rucellai's on Bees (1539) and Luigi Alemanni's on Cultivation (1546). The latter is the first true *Georgics* of the Renaissance. Alemanni wrote as an exile at the court of François I, and the scene now extended to France. His work was intended for practical use, and Virgil's also was widely treated as a handbook. But it was also admired as literature; and in Montaigne, who calls it 'the most accomplished work of poetry', it even takes precedence over the *Bucolics* and *Aeneid* as a source of quotations. Ronsard also imitated it and echoed it freely; but in him we find a tendency to concentrate on certain set pieces, primarily the eulogy of country life, the eulogy of Italy, the Aristaeus epyllion, the portents and civil war, the proems to Books 1 and 3 and the passage on sexual lust. These, with a few additions, comprise most of the knowledge of the *Georgics* shown by subsequent European, especially English, poets; and it is noteworthy that none of them comes from the ostensibly agricultural parts which together make up the bulk of the poem.

Three special kinds of poem stemmed largely from it: eulogies of rural life (based also on Horace's Second Epode, regardless of the fact that its conclusion tinges it with irony) – not the life of Virgil's working farmer but of the country gentleman, especially popular in the Netherlands; garden poems, notably René Rapin's in four books of Latin hexameters (1665), translated into English verse by John Gardiner (1706); and didactic poems on non-Virgilian subjects already exemplified by Fracastoro's *Syphilis* (1530) and poems on the rearing of silkworms by M. G. Vida (1527) and Thomas Moffat (1599). But in the sixteenth and seventeenth centuries the *Georgics* was still overshadowed by the *Bucolics* and *Aeneid*: it was only in the eighteenth century that it was to have its heyday.

This was ushered in, as to England, by the publication in 1697 of

Dryden's translation in heroic couplets; but the movement had already begun to spread all over Europe. Virgil's eulogy of Italy inspired other poets to praise their own land. Italy itself rediscovered Alemanni's poem, of which twenty-six editions were published between 1726 and 1781, and several rival 'géorgiques françaises' appeared. There were didactic poems on georgic subjects such as John Philips' *Cyder* (1706) and Dyer's *The Fleece* (1757). Descriptive poetry was now the rage. The most influential poem of the century for all Europe was James Thomson's *The Seasons*, and in successive revisions from 1726 to 1744 more and more was taken from Virgil's *Georgics*. Thomson helped to inspire in poetry Saint-Lambert's *Les Saisons* (1769), in music Haydn's *Seasons*, in painting landscapes such as Gainsborough's. Nature was the goddess, at first representing simply scenery, but later the creative power of the universe: *felix qui potuit . . .* was ascendant over *fortunatus et ille . . .* , and Thomson paraphrased the former passage (2.490–92) as the climax of his *Autumn*.

Meanwhile some agriculturalists such as 'Turnip' Townshend and William Benson, who translated *Georgics* 1 and 2 in 1724–5, at least thought of themselves as practising 'Virgilian husbandry'. But there was a heavy counter-attack, at least against 1.63–99, by Jethro Tull: 'I think it impossible for any scheme to be worse.' What is strange is that Virgil's recommendation of alternating crops should have been read for a thousand years before anyone seems to have tried what is now commonplace practice. Alternation is first heard of in the fourteenth century, but fallowing was still practised in some places even in the eighteenth.

The *Georgics* was present in every educated man's mind. William Pitt could adapt a passage from it inspiringly in the peroration of his speech (cited by T. E. Page) on the abolition of the slave trade, delivered on 2 April 1792 as the morning sun broke through the windows of the House of Commons:

Then also will Europe, participating in [Africa's] improvement and prosperity, receive an ample recompense for the tardy kindness – if kindness it can be called – of no longer hindering that continent from extricating herself out of the darkness which, in other more fortunate regions, has been so much more speedily dispelled –

nos . . . primus equis Oriens afflavit anhelis;
illic sera rubens accendit lumina Vesper.[1]

In the American colonies as well as Europe the *Georgics* was widely
read by educated people, especially in Dryden's translation, and in
the last decade of the eighteenth century it was among the specified
American college texts.[2]

But this great and only vogue of the *Georgics* did not survive the
disruption of leisured elegance by the *Sturm und Drang*, the French
Revolution, the Industrial Revolution and the Romantic Movement. In educated circles the Romans yielded to the Greeks, Virgil
to Homer. In Britain progressive urbanization has led to nostalgia
for country life in people sensitive to their environment. Victoria
Sackville-West's poem *The Land* (1926) had something of the
Virgilian spirit. An odd and rather macabre survival today is the
imposition of copying a Georgic as a regular punishment for
offending boys at Eton College. Finally, the number of translations that have appeared, though perhaps an acknowledgement of
the decline in ability to read Latin, is also a testimony of confidence
in the lasting appeal of the poem.

1. '. . . when the orient Sun with panting horses first breathes on us, for
them in the red of evening late Vesper lights his lamp.'(1.250–51)
2. D. M. Reinhold (ed.), *The Classic Pages* (1975), p. 6. For a fuller account
of the posthumous fortunes of the *Georgics* see L. P. Wilkinson, *The
Georgics of Virgil* (1969), chapter X.

Book 1 deals with field crops, mainly cereals, in its first half; the second half is more general. Virgil has Hesiod's *Works and Days* much in mind, and Aratus' *Diosemeia* in the long section on weather-signs; the influence of Lucretius is also apparent from time to time. He lays a Hesiodic emphasis on the necessity for constant hard work, and there are times when his view of life seems as pessimistic as Hesiod's:

> Toil mastered everything, relentless toil
> And the pressure of pinching poverty (145–6).
> . . . everything by nature's law
> Tends to the worse, slips ever backward, backward.
> As with a man who scarce propels his boat
> Against the stream: if once his arms relax,
> The current sweeps it headlong down the rapids (199–203).

The idea that earth itself tends to degenerate he will also have found in Lucretius (2.1138–80). There are many frustrations and occasional disasters. Yet the labour has its rewards too: Ceres looks down from heaven on the dedicated farmer; he can hope to see his barns full, and to enjoy 'the country's heavenly glory'. The diversification of life is a compensation for the hard work involved in material progress; and the rich variety of nature, reflected especially in the kaleidoscopic series of the weather-signs, is a pleasure to the observer.

Virgil begins with a summary, addressed to Maecenas, of the contents of the poem, brisk and businesslike. But he is already contriving, for the middle of the fifth line, an Eliotesque surprise: with a sudden heightening of the style he launches into an invocation, to the gods of the countryside and the young god-to-be, Caesar – two breathless dithyrambic flights of rhetoric which together comprise what is probably the longest period in Latin poetry. (For the contents of this proem see pp. 28; 26.) At the end of the Book, by reversing the order of Aratus' weather-signs so that moon and sun come last, he contrives that the sun leads (at 468) into a finale of equal élan, describing the portents and horrors of the civil wars that have devastated agriculture for more than a generation and again appealing to the gods, this time going back behind the Olympic pantheon imported from Greece to the ancient guardians of Rome, and praying that Caesar, 'this young man', may at last bring salvation to a ruined age. The Book is thus framed between two passages of high rhetoric which together comprise nearly 100 of its 514 lines. The tone of the first is buoyant, reflecting the situation when the poem was completed and Caesar was now supreme. That of the second is desperate, and seems, in its earlier part at least, to reflect the period several years earlier in which the poem was begun. The concluding simile, of the racing charioteer unable to control his chariot, parallels that of the rower unable to control his boat with which the first half of the Book concludes.

From the heady fantasies of the proem Virgil passes directly at 43 to his main subject, with advice on ploughing, choice of crops and maintenance of land. By the time we get to 70 we realize how this didactic matter may be the stuff of poetry. These first twenty-seven lines embody no more than four precepts: with rich soil plough early and deep; plough it more than once; with new land study climate and soil before deciding on its use; with poor soil turn it up lightly in autumn. But round these there is a rich embroidery of imagery: the mountain scene; the toiling bull and its ambitious master; the attribution of human feeling to an animal, and to fields and regions; and a whole series of images evoked by concrete instances – corn, vines, trees, pasture; saffron, ivory, incense, iron, musk; the romance of distant places; mythological allusion (to Deucalion). The approach is thoroughly personal, man to man. Hard work is a dominant theme. Some other themes will recur: distant lands, mythological figures, horses victorious at Olympia. The passage begins with ploughing and the bull and it comes round to these again at 63, thus exemplifying a device which Virgil learned from the Greeks for rounding off sections, 'ring-composition' as it has come to be called.

In the section that follows, on maintaining fertility (71–117), the distant lands theme is heard again (Mysia, Gargara), and that of religion appears (Ceres; praying for favourable weather), and the metaphor, which will also recur, of the farmer as a military commander of his fields.

A reference (118) to troubles caused by some animals and plants leads into a major passage, the 'theodicy' (121–47; see p. 28), after which we return to such troubles (147–59), again by ring-composition, which is exemplified again within this sub-section: oaks and acorns for food (148 and 159).

The description of the plough in 160–75 is a bow to Hesiod. Actually the Italian farmer would buy his plough: long ago Cato (135) had told him just where he could do so. To the technical details and the list of other implements Virgil 'adds honour' by an allusion to the implements that featured in the basically agricultural rites of the Mysteries celebrated at Eleusis, near Athens. The account of the threshing-floor in 176–86 reintroduces animal pests, this time with human touches – the tiny mouse constructing his granaries, the ant providing for her old age. The almond-tree at 187 is a foretaste of the prognostics that will come in later. The tendency of seeds to degenerate leads into the pessimistic passage already quoted, and the simile of the rower effectively concludes the first part of the Book, the 'Works'.

With a word meaning 'moreover' (*praeterea*), one of the hallmarks of Lucretius, Virgil bridges over the transition to his second part, 204 to 350, the 'Days'. He begins by telling when to sow what, not keeping to the chronological order of an almanack – his order is, in fact, autumn, spring, autumn, late autumn. Times are indicated by the rising and setting of constellations, beginning with Arcturus, already introduced at 68 in connection with ploughing. The Roman farmer would no doubt have a calendar to refer to, but reference to the stars was not obsolete (see Varro 1.28): it was, in any case, part of the literary tradition from Hesiod, and much more imaginative poetically. After 230 however the initial subject is almost lost in a series of admirable diversifications. The passage 231–58 on the zones of the sky, based on the Alexandrian scholar-poet Eratosthenes, subtly introduces the idea of Providence (231: 'This is the reason why . . .'; 238: 'by heavenly grace are granted . . .'), and also foreshadows the Prognostics (252: 'Thus we can forecast weather . . . thus the time to reap or sow, when best to . . . launch armadas . . .'), which brings us back by ring-composition to where we began at 204 ff.

There follows a series of genre pictures – what you can do in bad weather, what you may do on holy days. A short, archaic passage on lucky and unlucky days (276–86), another bow to Hesiod, a piece of literary opportunism in which Virgil varies the tradition with cavalier abandon, is followed by another of genre (287–310), in which the picture of man and wife doing odd jobs by the winter firelight leads on to a lively sequence of what you can do in winter (including the pleasures of entertainment, a foretaste of the rustic festival at 343–50). The culmination is a brilliant description of a surprise storm in summer (311–34), and the deduction that you must watch for weather-signs and above all observe the rites of the gods. This in turn leads into a sunny contrast after the dark storm, a description of a rustic festival which seems to be composite rather than individual – another reminder that the *Georgics* are literature, not a transcript of life. The way is thus prepared for the third part of the Book (351–514), the Prognostics or weather-signs given by Providence for the benefit of mankind.

The signs are largely taken from Aratus, with echoes of an interesting verse translation of him by Cicero and another, also lost, by Varro of Atax; but comparison enables us to observe Virgil's genius at work in applying imagination and expressive sensibility to what was largely a bare list. He begins with the signs of bad weather (351–92) and goes on to signs of good, both negative and positive (393–423). Then deftly, using the sun as connection, he passes to prognostics of human disaster, and so to the tremendous finale on the civil wars.

Note on the Translation

For a Penguin translation, even in verse, it has seemed appropriate to try to be 'faithful' to Virgil's text, though not in any slavish manner: to try to convey, as far as may be possible in English, not only the nuances of the sense and imagery and the expressiveness of the sounds, but also the movement of the verse. As vehicle I have decided on a loose, predominantly five-beat, metre which often streamlines itself into blank verse but which admits of variations such as the 'sprung' rhythm of Hopkins has made acceptable. A free use of 'feminine' endings has been designed to suggest the Latin hexameter, with its concluding spondee or trochee; and occasionally a shorter line has been used to adjust the movement of the English to that of the Latin.

A five-beat line does in fact represent the Latin hexameter as appropriately as a six-beat one, whether or not that is why blank verse has usually been favoured by English translators for this purpose. For there are good reasons for believing that the Romans read their poetry with the stress accent of their normal speech, the quantitative metre (originally Greek) being heard as a counterpoint or undercurrent; and the result is often a line of five stresses such as

altérnis ídem tónsas cessáre nováliś.[1]

Line references to the Latin text are given at ten-line intervals of the translation.

1. See L. P. Wilkinson, *Golden Latin Artistry* (1963), chapter 4 and appendix 1.

What makes the corncrops glad, under which star
To turn the soil, Maecenas, and wed your vines
To elms, the care of cattle, keeping of flocks,
All the experience thrifty bees demand –
Such are the themes of my song.
                              You brightest lamps
That lead the year's procession across the sky;
Liber and nurturing Ceres, since your grace
Procured that earth should change Chaonia's acorns
For the rich ears of grain, and grapes be found
For lacing cups of Acheloüs' water;   9
You too, the present help of farmers, Fauns
(Come, Fauns and Dryad maidens, dance together:
Yours are the gifts I sing); and you for whom
The earth, smitten with your great trident, first
Brought forth the champing horse, Neptune; and you,
Haunter of woods, for whom in Cea's brakes
Three hundred snow-white bullocks crop rich pasture;
Yourself, leaving the high Arcadian glades,
Your birthplace, Pan of Tegea, graciously
Draw near; Minerva who revealed the olive,   18
The boy-inventor of the curving plough,
Silvanus with a young uprooted cypress,
Come you; and all the gods and goddesses
Who love to guard the country, you who foster
New fruits unsown, and you who from the sky
Send down abundant showers upon the sown.
And you above all, you of the unknown future –
Whether some council of the gods will soon
Receive you, Caesar; or whether you may choose
To visit cities, succour lands, and be   25
Acknowledged over this wide world (your brow
Bound with a wreath ancestral, Venus' myrtle)
Author of fruits and potentate of seasons;

Or whether as deity of the boundless sea
You come, and sailors recognize alone
Your godhead, furthest Thulê be your slave,
And Tethys proffer all her waves for dowry;
Or whether, to reinforce the zodiac,
You bring to the slow months your added presence,
Where now a space between the Virgin gapes   33
And the Claws that chase her (already in your favour
The flaring Scorpion is drawing in his arms
To yield his usurpation in the sky) –
Be what you will (save that the Underworld
Hopes not for you as king, and never may
Such dread desire for kingship come upon you,
Though Greece is spellbound by the Elysian Fields
And Proserpine is loath to follow Ceres
Calling her back to earth);
But smooth my path, smile on my enterprise,   40
Pity with me the unguided steps of farmers,
Come forward, and learn already to answer prayer.

   In early spring, when the ice on the snowy mountains
Melts and the west wind loosens and crumbles the clods,
Then it's high time for my bull at the deep-driven plough
To groan, and the share to gleam with the furrow's polishing.
That field and that alone
Answers the prayer of the demanding farmer
Which twice has felt the sun and twice the cold;
Its superabundant harvests burst his barns.   49
But with untried land, before we cleave it with iron,
We must con its varying moods of wind and sky
With care – the place's native style and habit,
What crops the region will bear and what refuse.
Here corn will prosper better, there the grape,
Elsewhere young trees or greenery unbidden.
Look how Tmolus sends us its fragrant saffron,
India ivory, incense the soft Sabaeans,
But iron the naked Chalybes, Pontus the pungent

Musk, and Epirus mares for Olympic palms.   59
Nature imposed these everlasting covenants
From the first on certain regions, right from the time
When Deucalion over the empty spaces of earth
Cast those stones that produced the race of men –
A hard race. Up then, and if your soil is rich,
From the first months of the year let your stout bulls
Turn it over, and let the clods lie there
For dusty summer to bake with ripening suns;
But if your soil is poor, it will be enough
To furrow it lightly just as Arcturus is rising –   68
There, lest the flourishing crop be choked with weeds,
Here, lest the meagre moisture dry to a desert
    Harvested land in alternating fallow
You will let recover, crusting in idleness;
Or at another season sow with spelt
Fields you have stripped of beans with quivering pods,
Rich beans or slender vetch or bitter lupine
With its brittle haulm and rustling undergrowth.
True, flax can parch, and oats can parch, and poppies
Steeped in Lethaean slumber parch the earth;   78
Still, alternation's no great labour: only
Don't be ashamed to saturate dry soil
With rich manure, and scatter grimy ashes
Over exhausted ground.
Thus too by change of crops, fields can be rested
Without the thanklessness of untilled land.
Again, it often pays, when fields are cropless,
To fire the stubble with rapidly crackling flames –
Whether it is that hence the soil derives
Mysterious strength and nourishing enrichment;   86
Or that the fire burns out all noxiousness
And sweats out surplus moisture; or that the heat
Opens new paths and loosens hidden pores
To let the seedlings drink; or tightens rather
And closes gaping ducts, lest seeping rains
Or power of parching sun too fierce, or cold,

The north wind's penetrating cold, may blast them.
He greatly helps his land who takes a mattock
To break the sluggish clods, and drags bush-harrows –
Ceres looks down from heaven and rewards him –   90
He too who, having first upheaved the surface
In ridges, breaks them down with angled ploughshare,
And disciplines the acres he commands.

   Wet skies in midsummer and clear in winter
Farmers should pray for. Corn loves winter dust.
Fields revel in it: with tillage such as this
Mysia surpasses herself, and even Gargara
Marvels at her own harvest. What of him,
The man who casts his seed, then hand to hand
Harries the field, lays low the unfertile ranks   105
Of sand, then coaxes rivulets to follow
His hoe among the tilth? Who, when exhausted
The earth swelters with dying verdure, look,
Down from the brow of a sloping pathway tempts
A trickle that murmurs purling over the pebbles
To cool the parched-up ground? Or what of him
Who, lest the stalk droop with its weight of ears,
Grazes luxuriance while the blades are tender,
Scarce showing above the furrow? Or what of him
Who drains collected moisture from the marsh   114
With sandy sumps, especially when a river
In the treacherous months has swollen and overflowed
Usurping all the countryside with mud,
Whence tepid vapour steams from off the pools.

   And yet, for all the experience and all
The labour of men and oxen at the plough,
The wicked goose and those Strymonian cranes
Do mischief, and the bitter-fibred endive,
Or overhanging trees. The Father himself
Willed that the path of tillage be not smooth,   122
And first ordained that skill should cultivate
The land, by care sharpening the wits of mortals,
Nor let his kingdom laze in torpid sloth.

Before Jove's reign no tenants mastered holdings,
Even to mark the land with private bounds
Was wrong: men worked for the common store, and earth
Herself, unbidden, yielded all more fully.
He put fell poison in the serpent's fang,
Bade wolves to prowl and made the sea to swell,
Shook honey down from the leaves, hid fire away,   131
And stopped the wine that freely flowed in streams,
That step by step practice and taking thought
Should hammer out the crafts, should seek from furrows
The blade of corn, should strike from veins of flint
The hidden fire. Then first upon their backs
Rivers felt boats of hollowed alder, then
Mariners grouped the stars and gave them names,
Pleiads and Hyads and the radiant Bear,
Lycaon's daughter. Now was found the way
To snare wild beasts with nets and birds with lime   139
And cordon off wide coverts with rings of hounds.
One lashes a broad river with a cast-net
Probing the depths, another drags through the sea
His dripping trawl. Next hardened iron came
And the creaking saw-blade (for the earliest men
Split wood with wedges), and last the various arts.
Toil mastered everything, relentless toil
And the pressure of pinching poverty.

   First Ceres taught men how to turn the earth
With iron, when acorns now and arbute-berries   148
In the sacred wood were failing and Dodona
Scanted her sustenance. But soon the cornfields
Themselves became a labour: blighting mildew
Devoured the haulm; slothfully in the ploughland
The thistle reared its prickles. Crops are choked,
A shaggy growth comes up, of burrs and caltrops,
And amid the shining tilth the sorry darnel
And barren wild oats reign. So that unless
You harry the weeds with unrelenting mattock
And scare the birds with noise, and with your billhook   156

Cut back the branches overshadowing
Your ground, and pray to the gods for rain, alas
Too late you will eye your neighbour's ample store
And shake an oak in the woods to comfort hunger.

    Now for the weapons the hardy farmer needs,
Essential for the sowing and raising of crops:
The share first and the curved plough's heavy stock,
And the lumbering wains of the Eleusinian Mother,
Drags, threshing-sledges and back-breaking mattocks.
Then there's the humble wicker-ware of Celeüs,   165
Hurdles of arbute, and the winnowing fan,
The ritual fan of Iacchus. All these things
You must think about and lay in long ahead
If you hope to earn the country's heavenly glory.
While still in the woods an elm is trained by bending
With main force into the shape of a curving plough-beam.
To the stem of this an eight-foot pole is fastened,
Two pin-ears and a bifurcated sharebeam.
Cut in advance light linden for the yoke,
And a length of beech for the stilt, the rearward handle   174
That steers the undercarriage. Hang this timber
Over your hearth for smoke to season it.

    There's many an ancient precept I can tell you
If you can bear a tale of humdrum tasks.
A threshing floor must first be flattened out
With a heavy roller, kneaded, concreted
With binding chalk, lest weeds push up, and lest
It crumble into dust. Then you'll be mocked
By pests of every kind. The tiny fieldmouse
Will set up house and build his granaries   182
Under your floor, or sightless moles establish
Their dormitory there. In hollows lurk
The toad and all the countless curious beasts
That earth engenders; the weevil ravages
The biggest heap of corn; so does the ant
That fears a lean old age.
Mark too when many an almond-tree puts on

Her finery and droops her fragrant boughs:
If fruit abounds your corn will be abundant,
Great will the heat and great the grinding be;   190
But if a wealth of thick dark leaves prevails,
Alas, a wealth of chaff is all you'll thresh.
I have seen many a sower treat his seeds
With nitre first of all, or with black lees
Of olive-oil, hoping the beans within
Will swell to justify the specious pods
And quickly cook however small the fire;
And I have seen selected seeds, with care
Long tested, yet degenerate, unless
Man's effort picked the largest year by year.   199
So it is: for everything by nature's law
Tends to the worse, slips ever backward, backward.
As with a man who scarce propels his boat
Against the stream: if once his arms relax,
The current sweeps it headlong down the rapids.

Like
Rowing upstream,
if you let up 1x,
you go downstream
or over the edge.

Now for the stars. The phases of Arcturus,
The Kids, the gleaming Snake, must be observed
By us no less than those who, bound for home
Over the windswept waters, brave the Euxine
And the jaws beside Abydos' oyster-beds.   207
When Libra balances the hours of day
And sleep, the light and shade upon the globe,
Then set your oxen working, men, and sow
Your fields with barley, up to the very eve
Of winter's rains, the impracticable season.
Then too's the time to bury in the soil
Your seeds of flax and Ceres' poppy, then
High time to bend your back over the plough,
While the earth is dry enough, and clouds hold up.
Spring is the time for sowing beans, in spring   battle   215
You too, lucerne, are given to the crumbly furrows,
And millet also claims its annual care,
When with his gilded horns the dazzling Bull

Opens the year, and the Dog backs down before him.
But if for a crop of wheat or hardy spelt
You work your ground, intent on grain alone,
Wait until dawn is the Pleiads' setting-time
And the Cnossian star of the burning crown retires
Before you commit to the furrows their due of seeds,
Nor entrust too early to reluctant soil   223
A whole year's hopes. Many begin before
Maia has set, but them the looked-for crop
Deceives with mere wild oats. But if you choose
To sow vetch or the common kidney-bean
And deign to foster the Pelusian lentil,
Sure sign will be the setting of Boötes:
Start, and keep sowing right into the frosts.
   This is the reason why the golden Sun
Marks through the twelve Signs of the Zodiac
Fixed measures of the orbit-course he steers.   232
Five zones comprise the sky. One's ever ruddy
With blazing sun and ever scorched with fire.
Round this to right and left at either pole
Stretch blue ones, ice-bound, fraught with gloomy storm-clouds.
But in between two zones by heavenly grace
Are granted to frail mortals; and a path
Is cut through both obliquely for those Signs
To wheel their ordered way. The universe
Rises towards Scythia and the Rhipëän heights
Steeply, and sinks towards Libya and the South.   241
Above our heads the zenith ever towers,
Beneath our feet dark Styx and the nether ghosts
Behold the nadir.
Here the huge Serpent glides with sinuous coil
Around, and like a river parts the Bears,
'The Bears that fear to dip themselves in the Ocean.'
There either, so men say, Night, dead of Night,
Keeps silence, with a pall of thickest shadow,
Or Dawn returns from us and brings back day,
And when the orient Sun with panting horses   250

First breathes on us, for them in the red of evening
Late Vesper lights his lamp.
Thus can we forecast weather though the sky
Be doubtful, thus the time to reap or sow,
When best to impel the treacherous sea with oars
And launch armadas, when to fell the pine-tree.
For not in vain we watch the constellations,
Their risings and their settings, not in vain
The fourfold seasons of the balanced year.

Whenever wintry rain confines the farmer   259
Much he can do betimes that otherwise
He'll have to hurry when the skies have cleared.
Ploughmen beat sharp the blunted ploughshare point;
Troughs can be scooped from tree-trunks, flocks be branded
And heaps of corn be labelled. Some will sharpen
Two-pronged supports and stakes, others prepare
Amerian withes to tie the trailing vine.
Now weave the pliant basket of bramble-shoots,
Now roast your grain, now grind it on your millstone.
Even on holy days the laws of gods   268
And men permit some tasks: no scruple ever
Forbade to clear out runnels; make a fence
For crops, set traps for birds, burn briar-thickets,
Or dip the bleating flock in a stream for health:
Often the driver of a dawdling donkey
Will load its flanks with oil or low-grade fruit
On a holy day, and bring back home from town
A chiselled millstone or a lump of pitch.

The Moon herself has appointed lucky days
In this degree or that for various tasks.   276
Avoid the fifth: upon that day the Furies
And Hell's wan king were born; upon it Earth
With monstrous parturition spawned the giants,
Coeus, Iapetus and grim Typhoeus
And the brothers who conspired to pull down heaven.
(Thrice they endeavoured – think of it – to heave
Mount Ossa on Mount Pelion, and then roll,

Forests and all, Olympus onto Ossa.
Thrice with his bolt the Father razed that pile.)
For planting vines the seventeenth is lucky,   284
Also for catching steers to break them in
And fitting warp-threads to the loom. The ninth
Is good for runaway slaves but bad for thieves.
There are many tasks that best present themselves
In the cool of night, or when the Morning Star
Bedews the earth at sunrise. Night is best
For reaping earless haulm, and night is best
For mowing dry hay-meadows: no lack then
Of softening moisture. One there is I know
Who sits up late in winter and by firelight   291
With a sharp blade trims his torches, while his wife,
Singing to mitigate her drudgery,
Passes the piercing shuttle through the web,
Or boiling down sweet must over the hearth
Skims froth with a bunch of leaves from the bubbling cauldron.
But noonday heat is the time to reap the corn
Of sunburnt Ceres, and in the noonday heat
The threshing-floor takes dried-out ears to grind;
Remember, 'strip to plough and strip to sow'.
Winter's for holidays: when it's cold outside   300
Farmers enjoy their gains and give themselves
To mutual entertainment. Self-indulgent
Winter plays host and charms away their worries;
As, when a laden ship comes home to harbour,
The crew make merry and decorate its stern.
Yet even then's the time to gather acorns,
Olives, bay-berries, blood-red myrtle-berries,
Then to set snares for cranes, and nets for stags,
Or chase the long-eared hare, or fell the doe
Whirling your hempen Balearic sling,   309
When snow lies deep and rivers push the ice-packs.
    What need to tell of autumn's storms and stars,
Of dangers to guard against when days draw in
And summer mildens, dangers too when spring

Cascades in showers just as the arable
Bristles with serried cornblades and the ears
On the green stalks are swelling with milky grain?
But often even when the farmer was leading
The reapers into his golden fields, already
Stripping the barley-ears from the brittle stems,   317
I've seen the winds join battle all together
To tug, uproot and toss the pregnant harvest
All round, until the storm's dark whirlwind swept
The flimsy stalks and flying stubble away.
And often too a mighty host of waters
Invades the sky, and gathering from the deep
Clouds roll and roll together an ugly storm
Of murky rain. Down headlong falls the sky
In sheets; the glad fruits of the oxen's labours
Are washed away; dykes fill, low river-beds   326
Swell to a roaring torrent, and the sea
Foams with the seething of its estuaries.
The Father himself in the midmost night of cloud
Wields thunderbolts amain. The mighty earth
Quakes at that shock. The wild beasts all are fled
And mortal hearts worldwide are cowering. He
With flashing brand the mountains,
Athos or Rhodope or high Ceraunia,
Shatters. The blasts and massive rains redouble;
Huge gusts set forests groaning, beaches howling.   334
In fear of this observe the months and stars –
Where Saturn's chilly planet retreats, in what
Orbits of heaven Mercury's fire wanders.
Above all, worship the gods, and to great Ceres
Pay yearly ritual after sacrifice
On the pleasant grass, when winter is vanishing
At last and spring's set fair. Then are the lambs
Fat, and the wines most mellow, then to drowse
Is sweet and on the hillside shades are deep.
Let all your farmhands duly worship Ceres.   343
Mingle for her the honeycomb with milk

And wine, and lead the sacrificial victim
Three times for luck around the nursling crops
Escorted by the band of celebrants
And all your folk, who loudly call on Ceres
To grace their homes; and see that no one puts
The sickle to the ripened corn before,
In Ceres' honour, crowned with a wreath of oak,
He's trod a lumbering measure and uttered her hymns.

    And that we might be able by sure signs   351
To anticipate these things, the heats and rains
And winds that bring the cold, the Father himself
Ordained the monthly warnings of the moon,
The sign of south winds dropping, and how the farmer
Should learn by observation when to keep
His cattle near their stalls. When winds are stirring
Either the firths begin forthwith to roughen
With choppy waves, and on the mountain-heights
Dry cracking sounds are heard, or coasts afar
Echo confusedly and in the copses   359
Increasing whispers rustle. Now the wave
Can scarce refrain from buffeting ships' keels
When gulls fly swiftly landward from mid-ocean
Bearing their cries inshore, and cormorants
Sport on dry land, and the heron leaves her haunts
In the marsh to soar aloft above the clouds.
Often when winds are brewing stars are seen
To hurtle and glide downsky, leaving behind,
Against the dark, long trails of luminous white.
Often again you'll see blowing about   368
Light chaff and falling leaves, or a pair of feathers
Dancing a jig on the surface of a pond.
But when there's lightning in fierce Boreas' quarter
Or thunder in the halls of Zephyrus
And Eurus, all the countryside's aswim
With overflowing dykes, and out at sea
Every sailor reefs his dripping sails.
Rain never catches men without some warning:

Either its surge has driven the skyey cranes
Before it deep down valleys, or a heifer   375
Looked up to heaven and spread her nostrils wide
To catch the breeze, or round and round the pond
The twittering swallow has flitted, and in the mud
Frogs have struck up their ancient croaking protest.
Most often too, wearing a narrow path,
The ant has brought from out of her inmost sanctum
Her eggs, and a huge rainbow has stooped to drink,
And an army of rooks, evacuating their mess-ground
In massive column, have thickly clapped their wings.
The manifold birds of the sea, and those that love   383
To rummage in the pools of Asian Caÿster –
These too you may see douching their backs with spray
In eager sport, now charging the waves head-first,
Now racing into the water, just for fun,
Revelling in the joys of the shower-bath.
'Rain, rain,' the relentless raven calls full-throated
And stalks the shore in solitary state.
Even girls spinning their nightly stint of wool
Indoors, are made aware that a storm is coming
When they notice the oil is sputtering in their lamp   391
And mouldy fungus gathering on the wick.
Clear skies and suns returning after rain
By no less definite signs can be foreseen,
For then unblurred is the piercing light of the stars.
And as if unaided by her brother's beams
The rising Moon shines; nor do woolly fleeces
Pass trailing over the sky. The halcyons
Beloved of Thetis spread no longer ashore
Their wings to the warming sun, and unclean swine
Forget to rootle and toss their straw to pieces.   400
But the mists seek out low ground and rest on the plains;
And the owl on the roof-top watching the sun go down
Works at her ominous evensong in vain.
Nisus appears high in the limpid heavens
And Scylla pays for stealing his crimson lock:

Wherever she escaping cleaves the air
There fierce and hostile, whirring down the breeze,
Nisus pursues: where Nisus mounts the breeze
She swiftly still escaping cleaves the air.
Then rooks with narrowed throat three times or four   410
Repeat their muted caws, and high aloft
In their dormitories often by some strange
Gladness elated chatter among the leaves.
What joy, now rains are over, to revisit
Their infant brood and their beloved nests!
It's not, I believe, that heaven has granted them
Intelligence, and fate especial foresight,
But when the weather and the inconstant moisture
Of the atmosphere changes its course, and Jove
Wet with sou'westers thickens what up to now   418
Was rare, and rarifies what up to now
Was thick, the images of their minds are changed,
Their sense feels motions other than it felt
When winds were herding the clouds; hence all that consort
Of birds in the fields, that joy among the beasts,
And the rooks' exultant throats.
      But if you mark the scorching sun and mark
The moon's successive phases, then tomorrow
Never will catch you by surprise, nor nights
Treacherously serene. When first the moon   427
Mends her returning fire, if with dim horns
She embraces dusky air, abundant rain
For farmers and the ocean is in store.
But if her face betrays a maiden blush
Wind it will be: wind always brings a blush
To golden Phoebe. If at her fourth rising
(The surest sign) pure and with horns unblurred
She walks the sky, all the ensuing day
And all the days to be born until the close
Of the month will then be free of rain or winds,   435
And sailors safely landed pay their vows
To Glaucus, Panopea and Melicertes.

The sun too, both in rising and in withdrawing
Beneath the waves, will give you signs; the sun
Commands most certain signs, both those he brings
At break of day and when the stars are rising.
If hiding in cloud he wears his morning guise
Flecked, and the centre of his disc concave,
Beware of showers: the south wind, from the deep
Driving, bodes ill for trees and crops and herds.   444
If either at peep of day his rays pierce scattered
Through cloud-banks, or with pallid cheek Aurora
Rises to leave Tithonus' saffron bed,
Poorly, alas, the vineleaf will protect
The ripened grapes, such showers of myriad hail
Will dance their pattering tap-dance on the roof.
This too still more it will pay you to remember:
When, having spanned Olympus, he's departing
Often we see colours of varying hue
Wander across his face; purple means rain,   453
Flame-colour means east winds; but if the flecks
Begin to take a tinge of fiery red,
Then will you see a welter everywhere
Of winds and stormclouds both. (On such a night
Let no man bid me cast my cable loose
And put to sea.) But if his orb is clear
Both when he fetches and returns the day,
No need to fear such stormclouds; you will see
The forests waving in a clear north wind.
In sum, what nightfall has in store, and whence   461
The wind brings sunny clouds, and what the moist
Sou'wester plots, the sun will give you signs.
Who dares call Sun a liar? He it is
Who often warns of dark revolts afoot,
Conspiracy and cancerous growth of war.
He too, when Caesar fell, showed pity for Rome,
Hiding his radiant head in lurid gloom,
That a guilty age feared everlasting night.
Though other portents at that time were shown

On earth and sea, by ominous howling dogs   470
And inauspicious birds. How often we saw
Etna, asurge with cracking furnaces,
Hurling up balls of flame and molten rocks,
Boil over onto the fields of the Cyclopses. *ody s.?*
Germany heard from every corner of heaven
The clash of arms, strange tremors shook the Alps,
And a voice was widely heard through silent woods,
A mighty voice, and phantoms ghastly pale
Were seen at nightfall. Cattle (dare I tell it?)
Spoke; rivers ceased to flow and the earth gaped;   479
In temples ivories wept and bronzes sweated.
Eridanus, the king of rivers, burst
His banks in violent spate and washed away
Whole forests over all the countryside
And cattle with their stalls. At that same time
Sinister filaments constantly were found
Marring the entrails' omens, constantly
Springs ran with blood, and through the hours of darkness
High cities echoed with the howl of wolves.
Never did lightnings flash more frequently   487
From a clear sky, never so often blazed
Dire comets. So it was that a second time
Philippi saw the clash of Roman arms
With Roman arms, nor did it irk the gods
That twice Emathia and broad Haemus' plains
Should batten on our blood.
Surely a time will come when in those regions
The farmer heaving the soil with his curved plough   *farmer will*
Will come on spears all eaten up with rust   *uncover spears*
Or strike with his heavy hoe on hollow helmets,   *when plowing.*   496
And gape at the huge bones in the upturned graves.

Gods of our fathers, Heroes of our land,
And Romulus, and mother Vesta, guardian
Of Tuscan Tiber and Roman Palatine,
Do not prevent at least this youthful prince *Octavian*
From saving a world in ruins: long ago

Our blood has paid enough for the perjury
Of Troy's Laomedon. The courts of heaven,
Caesar, have long begrudged your presence here,
Complaining that you care for mortal triumphs;   504
For right and wrong change places; everywhere
So many wars, so many shapes of crime
Confront us; no due honour attends the plough,
The fields, bereft of tillers, are all unkempt,
And in the forge the curving pruning-hook
Is made a straight hard sword. Euphrates here,
There Germany is in arms, and neighbour cities
Break covenants and fight; throughout the world
Impious War is raging. As on a racecourse,
The barriers down, out pour the chariots,   512
Gathering speed from lap to lap, and a driver
Tugging in vain at the reins is swept along
By his horses and heedless uncontrollable car.

No honor for land.

Book 2 deals with trees, and mainly with the vine, no doubt partly because of its importance in Italian diet and the sophisticated care it requires, but more because it embodies the power symbolized by Bacchus, which can lift the human spirit above its humdrum norm. The labour involved is lighter than in the case of field crops: the Hard Work theme is heard less often – momentarily at 61–2, more insistently at 397–419. The overall tone is therefore one of relief after the more sombre Book 1; and the visual rewards of cultivation, 'the country's heavenly glory', mentioned incidentally at 1.168, are more emphasized – 'O what joy to plant all Ismarus with vines and clothe the great Taburnus with olives!', 'What a joy it is to view Cytorus surging with its boxwoods and Naryx with its pines!'

On the other hand this Book has more prosaic detail than the others, more of what are basically catalogues. At times, indeed, Virgil is treading closely in the prose footsteps of Theophrastus. He is clearly aware of the danger of tedium and takes steps to avoid it. Wishing, for instance, to begin with nine ways of propagating trees, he does not simply prefix his list to the *seriatim* treatment of them: instead he sandwiches it into a divided proem, addressed to Bacchus (1–8) and to Maecenas (39–46), and proceeds thereafter. He assures Maecenas (42–4) that he will not attempt to be exhaustive. With his usual resourcefulness he succeeds in enlivening his subject.

In the first place, there are fine set-pieces (see below). Then there are shorter vignettes – the scene of sacrifice (192–4); the army drawn up for battle (a simile elaborated in Homeric fashion beyond its relevance, for pictorial effect, 279–84); the plantation fire (303–11); the Attic and Italian village festivals (380–96). There are topical glimpses of localities – Mantua, wounded by the evictions, with the snow-white swans on its reedy river; Acerrae inundated by the river Clanius. Occasional touches maintain the religious aura. There is something numinous about trees, as about rivers – oaks sacred to Jupiter, 'the Chaonian Father', Hercules' poplar, Minerva's olive, beloved also of Peace; Mars on the field of battle; and finally the gods of the countryside – Pan, Silvanus and the

Nymphs. Bacchus is everywhere, especially at the rural festival (385–96), which balances that of Ceres at 1.338–50. At 229 these two are dragged in almost superfluously.

By variety of every kind impetus is maintained. Life is also imparted ubiquitously by the attribution of human feelings to plants and inanimate things, most notably in the wine catalogue (89–102), where hierarchy of vintages and their individual pride is respected. The theme of the different produce of countries (1.56 –9) is expanded here at 114–35 to lead into the praise of Italy, with which those countries cannot vie (136–76). There were eulogies of Italy, with its variety, fertility and temperate climate, in contemporary prose works, notably in Varro (1.2.6). We have here an exhilarating set-piece ranging far beyond the sphere of agriculture and sometimes even of sober truth. This is the land where Saturn once reigned, before Jupiter introduced the disciplining régime of hard labour.

The impetus of this passage carries us on through mundane ones concerned with varieties of soil (177–258) and the care of trees, especially vines (259–457). Though this long tract has only one set-piece to relieve it, the rhapsody on spring (323–45), Virgil takes every opportunity to avoid tedium. The olive and other trees are treated very perfunctorily compared with the vine (420–57). They require much less care, and so lead up suitably to the long and famous eulogy of country life which is the climax of the Book, where the helpfulness of nature is emphasized. This again is a rhetorical set-piece. The theme had recently been treated briefly by Lucretius (2.20–36), and was already so much of a commonplace that Horace, in his Second Epode, could guy it by presenting a virtuoso version and then revealing, in a brief *dénouement*, that the speaker is an insincere city financier. Virgil's version is constructed round three main contrasts – city luxury and country sufficiency (467–74); scientific rationalism (475–83; 490–92) and knowing the gods of the country (483–9, 493–502); worldly ambition and innocent country pursuits (513–40). See pp. 37–8.

There is one trace in this passage of the atmosphere of Book 1, in the undemanding youth inured to hard work (472); but otherwise the whole conception is incompatible with it, that of the earth of its own accord lavishing on the countryman an easy livelihood (especially 459–60, 500–501). The dream is that of an educated townsman longing for leisurely rest in broad acres or in the cool shade of Thessaly and that archetypal beauty-spot the vale of Tempe, and romanticizing about the Bacchic revels of Spartan girls on Mount Taygetus (467–71). This is the world of the *Bucolics*, not of the rest of the *Georgics*; a world of escape. It is the dispensation of Saturn, the opposite of that of Jupiter which superseded it in the theodicy in Book 1 (121–46), and we are explicitly reminded of the fact at 536–8 (see p. 28).

Book 2

Thus far my song has been of tilth below
And stars above; now, Bacchus, it shall be
Of you, and with you of the woodland saplings
And the rearing of the slow-maturing olive.
Come, Father of the Winepress: yours are the gifts
That here abound; for you the land burgeons
Pregnant with vine-leafed autumn, and the vats
Foam to the brim. Come, Father of the Winepress,
Swiftly pull off your buskins and with me
Dip your bare legs deep in the new must.   8

First, trees know various ways of propagation.
Some grow of their own accord with no control
Of human hand: across the plains, along
The winding river-banks they hold their sway,
The yielding osier and the pliant broom,
The poplar and the willow silvery-leaved.
Some spring from fallen seed, the lofty chestnut,
The oaks whose foliage dominates the groves
Of Jove and those the Greeks deemed oracles.
In some, thick undergrowth sprouts from the root,   17
Cherries and elms; Apollo's Delphic bay-shoot,
Tiny beneath its mother's massive shelter,
Crops up. These methods nature first provided
For trees and shrubs and sacred groves to flourish.
In others, man's experience as he goes
Has found a way: one tearing suckers from
The mother's tender body buried them
In furrows; another planted in the ground
Pieces of stem split crosswise at the end
Or sharpened stakes. Some trees await the arch   25
Of down-bent layers, offshoots still deriving
Life from their parent soil. Others require
No root: the pruner cuts unhesitating

The topmost spray to entrust to earth again.
Why, even from an olive trunk sawn through,
Strange to relate, dry wood can put down roots.
And often we observe how one tree's branches
Can turn, with no harm done, into another's —
Pear trees transformed to bear engrafted apples
And plum trees red with the fruit of stony cornels. 34

   Come, farmers, then, and learn the form of tendance
Each kind of tree requires; domesticate
The wild by culture. Do not let your land
Lie idle. O what joy to plant with vines
All Ismarus and clothe the great Taburnus
With olives!
          And you, Maecenas, lend your aid,
My pride, the better part of all my glory.
Set sail with me on this my enterprise,
Wing swiftly out to sea. I cannot hope
To scour in verses all the wide expanse — 42
'Not if I had a hundred mouths and tongues
And a throat of iron.' Lend your aid, to cruise
Coastwise and close inshore. I'll not detain you
With fancy myths, digressions, long preambles.

Won't be exhaustive

   The trees that lift themselves spontaneously
Into the realms of light are blithe and strong,
For power is in the soil, but prove unfruitful.
Yet even these, if grafted or transplanted
To the care of well-dug trenches, will discard
Their wildwood spirit and by discipline 51
Be trained, whatever role you care to teach them,
To learn it gladly. Then again the sucker
That rises barren from the stem low down
Will do the same if planted out well spread
In open ground; if left, its mother's branches
And overshadowing foliage will bereave it
Of offspring, parch its bearing in the bud.

The tree that rears itself from fallen seed
Grows slowly, though some day your children's children
Will find its shade rewarding, and its fruit   58
Degenerates, forgetting its old flavour.
Vines of this sort bear sorry clusters, fit
Only for hungry birds.
            The moral is
That every tree needs labour, all must be
Forced into furrows, tamed at any cost.
But olives favour truncheons, vines come best
From layers, myrtles best from solid stems,
From suckers hardy hazels, and from seed
The mighty ash, the shady tree whose leaves   66
Hercules plucked to crown him, and the acorns
Of the Chaonian Father. Likewise spring
From seed the lofty palm tree and the fir
Destined to see the hazards of the deep.
Grafting it is that makes the rugged arbute
Bear walnuts, barren planes rear healthy apples
And chestnuts foster beeches; thanks to this
The manna-ash can blanch with pear-blossom
And pigs munch acorns at the elm tree foot.

   The arts of budding and of grafting differ.   73
In the former, where the buds push out of the bark
And burst their delicate sheaths, just in the knot,
A narrow slit is made. In this an eye
From an alien tree is set and taught to merge
Into the sappy rind.
In the latter, knotless trunks are trimmed, and there
Wedges are driven deep into the wood,
Then fertile slips inserted. Presently
Up shoots a lofty tree with flourishing boughs,
Marvelling at its unfamiliar leaves   82
And fruits unlike its own.

   Again, there are different kinds of sturdy elm,
Willow and lotus and Idaean cypress;
Of oily olive too – the oval orchas,

79

The long-shaped radius, and the pausia
Gathered still bitter. Different kinds of apple
Alcinoüs' orchards grew. Pears also differ –
The Crustumerian and the Syrian
And the rotund voluma. Grapes that hang
From our Italian vines are not the same   89
As those of Lesbos that Methymna harvests.
Thasian vines there are and white Mareotic;
These like a richer, those a lighter soil.
Psithian is best for raisin-wine, Lageian
Subtle, to test the legs and tie the tongue.
Precocious wines and Purples and – but how,
Rhaetic, can I do justice to your merits?
Yet even so, beware of challenging
Falernian cellars. Aminnēan vines
Produce a wine uncommonly full-bodied: 97
Tmolian and even imperial Phanaean
Stand in its presence; while the Lesser Argite
Finds no competitor for sheer abundance
And lasting quality. Nor must I fail,
Rhodian, to mention you, acceptable
To the gods and with dessert, nor you, Bumastan,
With clusters well endowed. But numberless
Are the varieties and vintage-names,
And why attempt to count them? Sooner count
How many grains of sand the west wind whirls   106
Across the Sahara, or how many waves,
When the east wind falls savagely on shipping,
Come in to break on the Adriatic shore.
   Neither can every soil bear everything.
By rivers willows grow, in heavy marshland
Alders, on rocky mountains barren ashes.
Shores greatly favour myrtles. Finally
Bacchus loves open hillsides, yews the cold
The north wind blows. And cast your eyes abroad
To the furthest cultivators in the world,   114
The eastward-dwelling Arabs and the painted

Gelonians: each nation has its trees –
India alone black ebony, frankincense
Saba alone. What need to tell of balsams
Dripping from fragrant branches, or the berries
Of Egypt's evergreen acacia,
Of Ethiopia's cotton-white plantations
And the Chinese combing fleecy silk from leaves?
Or India's jungles, nearer to the Ocean,
The farthest corner of the world, where none   123
Can shoot an arrow clear above the treetops
(And no mean archers are that Indian race)?
From Media comes the sour and lingering taste
Of the citron, promptest remedy to drive
The deadly poison from the limbs of one
Whose wicked stepmother has drugged his drink.
The tree itself is large, and in appearance
Much like a bay – could be indeed a bay
But for the different scent it wafts around.
No wind shakes down its leaves; its blossom too   133
Tenacious in the extreme. The Medes employ it
To cure bad breath and treat old men for asthma.

But neither Media's land most rich in forests,
The gorgeous Ganges or the gold-flecked Hermus
Could rival Italy; not Bactria
Nor India nor that rich Arabian isle
Panchaïa with its incense-bearing sands.
Here have no bulls with nostrils breathing fire
Ploughed at the sowing of a dragon's teeth
For a human harvest bristling rank on rank   142
With spears and helmets. But the land is full
Of teeming fruits and Bacchus' Massic liquor.
Olives are everywhere and prosperous cattle.
From here the war-horse comes that charges proudly
Over the plain; from here your milk-white herds,
Clitumnus, and the bull, greatest of victims,
Plunged often in your sacred stream, that lead

Triumphant Romans to the Capitol.
Here is perpetual spring, and summer weather
At other times. Twice yearly cattle breed,   150
Twice orchards give us crops. But ravening tigers
And broods of savage lions are not found,
Nor monkshood to delude the wretch that picks it;
Nor does the scaly snake writhe over the ground
Huge sinuous curves to gather such great length
And rear it in a coil. And then the cities,
So many noble ones raised by our labours,
So many towns we've piled on precipices,
And rivers gliding under ancient walls.
What of the seas, the Upper and the Lower,   158
That wash our shores? What of the Great Lakes,
You, mightiest Larius, and you, Benācus,
Surging with waves and roaring like the sea?
What of the harbours and the Lucrine barrage
And ocean loud with indignation seething
Where far the baffled Julian waves resound
And Tyrrhene tides flow channelled into Avernus?
This land can boast of silver in her veins
And copper mines, has flowed with streams of gold.
The same has bred a vigorous race of men,   167
Marsians, the Sabine stock, Ligurians
Inured to hardship, Volscians javelin-armed,
And heroes, Decii, Marii, Camilli,
Scipios, stubborn fighters, and you, Caesar,
Greatest of all, who now victoriously
In Asia's farthest bounds are fending off
Unwarlike Indians from our Roman strongholds.
Hail, mighty mother of fruits, Saturnian land,
And mighty mother of men. For you I broach
These themes of ancient fame and ancient skill,   174
Bold to unseal a sacred fount, and sing
The song of Ascra through the towns of Rome.

Now for the characters of various soils,
Their strength, their colour and their qualities
For bearing produce. First, the churlish kind
On grudging hills – lean clay, pebbles and scrub –
Welcomes the long-lived olive-trees of Pallas.
You'll recognize it by the outcrop there
Of numerous wild olives, all the ground
Strewn with their berries. But the soil that's rich,   183
Blessed with sweet moisture, level land that's lush
With herbage, teeming with fertility
(Such as we often see when looking down
On a valley in the mountains, whither torrents
From crags above bring down a wealth of mud),
Or southward-facing hillsides apt to breed
The bracken hated by the curving plough –
Such land one day will yield you vines most potent,
With Bacchus overflowing, rich in grapes,
Rich in the liquid poured from golden vessels   192
When, at the altar where the stout Etruscan
Blows on his ivory pipe, on spacious dishes,
We offer reeking entrails to the gods.

"scene of sacrifice"

   But if your preference is for herds of cattle
Or breeding sheep, or goats that damage plants,
Go seek the distant glades of rich Tarentum
Or pasture such as hapless Mantua lost
That feeds white swans upon its reedy river.
There will your flocks lack neither grass nor water,
And all that your herds have cropped the long day through   201
In one short night the chilly dew will restore.
   Earth that is black and, when you drive your share in,
Looks rich, and crumbly soil (the aim of ploughing)
Is mainly best for corn; no other land
Sees straining oxen draw more waggons home;
Or land from which the impatient husbandman
Has carted off the timber he has felled,
Woods that have long been idle, ancient homes
Of birds, uprooted; they, their nests abandoned,

Posts abandoned?

Fly upward, but the rough new land below   211
Begins to gleam in the wake of the driven plough.
The starveling gravel found in hilly country
Scarcely provides enough of humble spurge
And rosemary for bees. The porous tufa
And chalk eroded by black watersnakes
Claim that no land gives serpents such sweet food
Nor refuge in such labyrinthine lairs.
Land which exhales thin wisps of fleeting vapour,
Which draws in moisture and at will expels it,
Which always clothes itself with its own verdure   219
And harms no iron with scurf or salty rust –
That will entwine your elms with lusty vines,
That grows rich olives, that you'll find in practice
Both kind to flocks and yielding to the share.
Such land rich Capua ploughs, the coast beneath
Vesuvius' shoulder, and the banks of Clanius,
That persecutor of forlorn Acerrae.
    How to distinguish soils I now will tell you.
If you want to know whether a soil is light
Or heavier than most (the one is friendly   227
To grain, to grapes the other – heavy to Ceres,
Light to Lyaeus), first you must select
A fitting place, then have a pit dug deep
Into the solid ground. Replace the earth
And stamp the surface down. If more is needed
To fill the hole, it's light and fit for pasture
And genial vines; but if it won't go in
And when the hole is full there's earth to spare,
It's heavy: be prepared for clinging clods
And stubborn ridges; plough with sturdy oxen.   237
For salty soil, 'sour' as the farmers call it
(Unfruitful, unamenable to ploughing –
Wines lose their breeding, apples their distinctions),
Here is a test: take down from your smoky rafters
Wine-strainers and close-woven wicker baskets.
Mix in them that bad earth with sweet spring-water

84

And press it down to the full; the moisture then
Will struggle through the mesh in bulging drops.
Taste it: the sourness will be manifest
In the wry grimace of anyone who tries it.   245
For richer soil the final test is this:
It never crumbles in your hands when kneaded
But sticks like pitch between your clutching fingers.
Wet soil, unduly lush, produces verdure
Too rank. From prodigal fertility
Preserve us, and from boast of too much strength
When the ears are young! The heavy and the light
Silently, by mere weight, betray themselves.
The black – or any colour – you can tell
At a glance; but to detect the treacherous coldness   256
Is hard, your sole occasional informers
Pitch-pines or guilty yews or dark green ivy.

  These points observed, remember long ahead
To bake the earth, demolishing the peaks
With trenches, and expose the upturned clods
To the cold north wind, before you plant in it
The cheerful stock of vines. A crumbly soil
Is best – the winds and frosts will see to that
And a burly digger to upheave your acres.
But men who have an eye to every detail   265
Seek out a nursery, where the tender crop
May first be educated for the trees,
Akin to that destined for its transplanting,
Lest sudden change to an alien foster-mother
Worry the nurslings. Further, to preserve
The stance of each to the quarters of the sky,
They sign its bark to show which side has faced
The southern heat, which turned its back on the pole:
So much effect has habit on the young.

  Determine first whether to site your vineyard   273
On hill or level. If it's rich plain-land
You're laying out, plant closely: in close order
Bacchus is no less hearty; but if uneven

With mounds, or sloping hillside, give your ranks
Plenty of freedom. None the less exactly
Each avenue between the trees must square
With each cross-path. As when for a full-scale battle
A marching column has halted in the field,
And the legion has deployed in line its cohorts,
And the ranks are dressed, and far and wide the landscape 281
Ripples with gleaming bronze – the ragged mêlée
Is not yet joined, but in between the armies
Mars wavers undecided – so let all
Your vineyard be drawn up in regular
Formation, rank and file spaced equally,
Not for the idle pleasure of the eye
Alone, rather because not otherwise
Can the earth bestow an equal potency
On all, and the boughs have room to spread themselves.

army for
ready for
battle

    How deep should be your digging? I would risk 288
Entrusting vines to a quite shallow furrow.
But trees are planted deep down in the earth,
Oak above all, whose root approaches Hell
As nearly as its top approaches Heaven.
Therefore no storms nor hurricanes uproot it:
Unmoved, triumphant, it survives the passing
Of many sons and centuries of men,
While mighty in the midst it spreads afar
Its branches, and sustains a massive shade.

    Nor let your vineyards slope towards the sunset, 298
Nor intersperse your vines with hazel trees,
Nor seek the highest shoots and take your cuttings
From the top of the tree (vines love the earth too much),
Nor hurt the young by using a blunt knife.
Do not insert wild olives, for a shepherd
Often unwittingly lets fall a spark
Which lurks beneath the oily bark at first
Unseen, then grasps the wood and shooting up
To the higher foliage sends a mighty roar
Skyward, advances next victoriously 306

Fire

Along the boughs and lords it over the treetops,
Wrapping the whole plantation in flames and shooting
A thick black cloud of pitchy murk to heaven,
Especially if a gale has swooped on the woods
To gather and sweep along the conflagration.
When this occurs, the vines have no more strength
In their stock, no hope that, if they are cut back,
They may revive and flourish from the ground:
Wild olives, bitter-leaved, alone survive.

   And let no wiseacre, however specious,   315
Induce you to disturb the hardened ground
When the north wind is blowing. Then the cold
Of winter grips the fields, and nothing sown
Can fasten in the earth a frozen root.
Best time for planting is the flush of spring
When the white bird, the bane of trailing snakes,
Appears; or close upon the frosts of autumn,
When summer's waning but the fiery steeds
Of the sun have yet to reach the Signs of winter.
Spring is the friend of woods, spring is the friend   323
Of forest leaves, in spring the country swells
Clamouring for the fertilizing seeds.
Then the almighty father Heaven descends
Into the lap of his rejoicing bride
With fecund showers, and with her mighty body
Mingling in might begets all manner of fruits.
Then are wild thickets loud with singing birds
And in their season herds renew their loves
The nurturing earth is pregnant; warmed by breezes
Of Zephyrus the fields unloose their bosoms.   331
Mild moisture is all-pervading, and unharmed
The grasses brave the unaccustomed suns;
Nor do the vine-shoots fear a southern gale,
Or northern rainstorms driving down the sky,
But put forth buds and all their leaves unfold.
Days such as these shone out and went their way,
I can well believe, at the dawn of the infant world:

Springtime it was, the great globe celebrated
Spring, and the east winds spared their wintry blasts,
When cattle first drank in the light, and man,   340
The earthborn race, first reared his head in the fields,
And wild beasts were let loose to roam the forests
And stars to roam the sky. Nor would the stress
Of life be bearable for tender things
Did not so long a respite come between
The cold and heat, and heaven's indulgence grant
This comfort to the world.

   For the rest, whenever you plant your shoots, be sure
To spread rich dung around and bury them
In plenty of earth; and dig in pebbles for drainage   348
Or jagged shells: water will thus seep in
Between them, and thin exhalations rise,
And the crops pluck up their spirits. There have been
Those who have covered them with a lid of stone
Or a massive pot, protection both from downpours
And when the torrid Dogstar cracks the fields.

   The seedlings planted, it remains to loosen
The earth around their stems repeatedly,
Plying your two-pronged hoe, or work the soil
By driving in the plough and even steering   356
Your straining oxen in between the vine-rows.
Make ready then supports, the rods you peel
Smooth as a spear-shaft, next the stakes of ash
And sturdy bifurcated props whose strength
Will aid the vines to clamber and learn to scorn
The winds, and scale their climbing-frame of elm
Storey by storey, right to the very top.

   When they are just beginning to grow up,
Their leaves still fresh, be gentle to the young;
And when the sprig is racing merrily   364
Unbridled through the air do not as yet
Submit it to cold steel, but cull the leaves
Selectively, using your fingernails.
Later, when they are quite grown up, embracing

[margin annotation:] false victory?

The elms with lusty stems, then crop their leaves,
Then amputate their branches (earlier
They cannot bear the knife), then exercise
Hard discipline and curb the straggling branches.
   Fences must also be woven, to keep out
All beasts, especially while the leaves are tender,   372
Still unprepared for trouble; for besides
Winter's unkindness and the sun's oppression
Wild buffaloes and nagging goats forever
Make sport of them, and sheep and greedy heifers;
And neither gripping cold with icy hoar-frost
Nor sultry summer brooding on dry rocks
Harm them so much as do those herds, the poison
Of those sharp teeth, the bite that scars the stem.
For this same crime the he-goat's sacrificed
To Bacchus on every altar; so the ancients   381
Began the staging of plays, and Theseus' sons
At crossroads and in villages gave prizes
For local talent, and tipsy on the green
Cavorted on greasy goatskins. Even thus
The Ausonian farmers, sprung from Trojan pilgrims,
Make sport with uncouth verses and ribald laughter
And don horrific masks of hollowed bark,
And call upon you, Bacchus, in cheerful songs,
Suspend for you small effigies of wool
High on a pine. Hence every vineyard ripens   390
With generous fruit, the valleys and deep glades
And every place to which the god has turned
His comely countenance are filled with plenty.
To Bacchus, then, we'll duly pay our worship
In ritual hymns, with offerings of dishes
And cakes; and led by the horn the damnèd he-goat
Will stand beside the altar, and we'll roast
The fatty flesh on spits of hazel-wood.
   This further task there is in raising vines,
One that is never-ending: every year   398
Three times or four the soil must be reopened,

[margin handwritten: description of Attic + Italian village festivals]

Clods broken everlastingly with the back
Of two-pronged hoes, and the whole plantation freed
Of leaves. The farmer's labour is a treadmill:
All round the year he treads in his own tracks.
At the very moment when the vine has shed
Its latest leaves and the cold north wind has shaken
The glory from the woods, at that same moment
The lively husbandman projects his thoughts
Into the coming year, with Saturn's hook   406
Goes after the vine just left, to shear and shape it.
Be first to dig the ground, be first to burn
Your carted prunings, first to store your props;
Be last to harvest. Twice in the year the shade
Threatens the vines, twice weeds and undergrowth
Sprawl over the ground, both causing heavy labour.
'Praise large estates but cultivate a small one.'
Again, there's cutting of rough butcher's broom
In the woods and rushes on the banks of rivers,
And the wild willow-bed demands attention.   415
At last the vines are bound, their trees at last
Release the pruning-knife, the last vine-dresser
Bursts into song to tell his rows are finished.
Yet still you must harass the earth and stir the dust
And fear Jove's downpour for your ripening grapes.

  Olives, by contrast, call for little tendance:
They don't expect the sickle or gripping drag-hoe
Once they have taken hold in the field and weathered
The breezes. Once the earth has been opened up
By the curving fang it will, with the plough's assistance, 423
Provide sufficient moisture to swell the fruit.
Thus you can raise plump olives, pride of Peace.
  Fruit-trees, as soon as they feel their trunks are sturdy
And know their strength, push swiftly towards the stars
By inborn force, needing no help from us.
And likewise every wood is laden with fruit,
The birds' wild haunts blushing with crimson berries.

Shrub trefoil serves for browsing, while the forest
Supplies the brands that feed nocturnal fires
And spread the light around. With nature's lead   432
Shall man be slow to plant and pay with trouble?
And, grander trees apart, the humble broom
And willows there provide both feed for flocks
And shade for shepherds, fences for sown fields
And provender for bees. What a joy it is
To view Cytorus surging with its boxwoods
And Naryx with its pines! What a joy it is
To look on land beholden to no drag-hoes
Nor any human care! Even the barren
Forests that grow high up on Caucasus   440
For ever tossed and torn by angry blasts
Of Eurus, yet yield each some useful product –
Pines for ships' timbers, cedars and cypresses
For building houses; thence supplied, men turn
Spokes for the farmer's wheels and drums for his waggons
And lay down keels for boats. The willow's wealth
Is osiers, elms give foliage, while the myrtle
And warrior cornel breed tough shafts for spears
And yews are bent for Ituraean bows.
Smooth lime as well and box the lathe has shaved   449
Are shaped and chiselled out, and the buoyant alder
Launched on the Po swims in its turbid current,
And bees set up their hives in hollow cork-trees
Or the heart of a rotten holmoak. What so worthy
Of praise has Bacchus brought us? Bacchus' gifts
Have even led to crime; for he it was
Who tamed in death the liquor-maddened Centaurs,
Rhoetus and Pholus and Hylaeus, him
Who menaced the Lapiths with a massive wine-bowl.

    How lucky, if they know their happiness,   458
Are farmers, more than lucky, they for whom,
Far from the clash of arms, the earth herself,
Most fair in dealing, freely lavishes

An easy livelihood. What if no palace
With arrogant portal out of every cranny
Belches a mighty tide of morning callers
And no one gapes at doors inlaid so proudly
With varied tortoiseshell, cloth tricked with gold
And rare Corinthian bronzes? What if wool
Is white, not tainted with Assyrian poison,   465
And honest olive oil not spoilt with cassia?
Yet peace they have and a life of innocence
Rich in variety; they have for leisure
Their ample acres, caverns, living lakes,
Cool Tempês; cattle low, and sleep is soft
Under a tree. Coverts of game are there
And glades, a breed of youth inured to labour
And undemanding, worship of the gods
And reverence for the old. Departing Justice
Left among these her latest earthly footprints.   474

  For my own part my chiefest prayer would be:
May the sweet Muses, whose acolyte I am,
Smitten with boundless love, accept my service,
Teach me to know the paths of the stars in heaven,
The eclipses of the sun and the moon's travails,
The cause of earthquakes, what it is that forces
Deep seas to swell and burst their barriers
And then sink back again, why winter suns
Hasten so fast to plunge themselves in the ocean
Or what it is that slows the lingering nights.   482
But if some chill in the blood about the heart
Bars me from mastering these sides of nature,
Then will I pray that I may find fulfilment
In the country and the streams that water valleys,
Love rivers and woods, unglamorous. O to be
Wafted away to the Thessalian plains
Of the Sperchēus, or Mount Taÿgetus
Traversed by bacchant feet of Spartan girls!
O who will set me down in some cool glen
Of Haemus under a canopy of branches?   489

92

Blessèd is he whose mind had power to probe
The causes of things and trample underfoot
All terrors and inexorable fate
And the clamour of devouring Acheron;
But happy too is he who knows the gods
Of the countryside, knows Pan and old Silvanus
And the sister Nymphs. Neither the people's gift,
The fasces, nor the purple robes of kings,
Nor treacherous feuds of brother against brother
Disturb him, not the Danube plotting raids   497
Of Dacian tribesmen, nor the affairs of Rome
And crumbling kingdoms, nor the grievous sight
Of poor to pity and of rich to envy.
The fruit his boughs, the crops his fields, produce
Willingly of their own accord, he gathers;
But iron laws on tablets, the frantic Forum
And public archives, these he has never seen.
Some vex with oars uncharted waters, some
Rush on cold steel, some seek to worm their way
Into the courts of kings. One is prepared   504
To plunge a city's homes in misery
All for a jewelled cup and a crimson bedspread;
Another broods on a buried hoard of gold.
This one is awestruck by the platform's thunder;
That one, enraptured, gapes at the waves of applause
From high and low rolling across the theatre.
Men revel steeped in brothers' blood, exchange
The hearth they love for banishment, and seek
A home in lands beneath an alien sun.
The farmer cleaves the earth with his curved plough.   513
This is his yearlong work, thus he sustains
His homeland, thus his little grandchildren,
His herds and trusty bullocks. Never a pause!
The seasons teem with fruits, the young of flocks,
Or sheaves of Ceres' corn; they load the furrows
And burst the barns with produce. Then, come winter,
The olive-press is busy; sleek with acorns

The pigs come home; the arbutes in the woods
Give berries; autumn sheds its varied windfalls;
And high on sunny terraces of rock   522
The mellow vintage ripens.
Meanwhile his darling children hang upon
His kisses; purity dwells in his home;
His cows have drooping udders full of milk,
And in the fresh green meadow fatling kids
Spar with their butting horns. The master himself
Keeps holiday, and sprawling on the grass,
With friends around the fire to wreathe the bowl,
Invokes you, Lord of the Winepress, offering
Libation, and nails a target to an elm   530
For herdsmen to compete in throwing darts,
While hardy rustic bodies are stripped for wrestling.
Such was the life the ancient Sabines lived
And Remus with his brother; thus it was
That Rome became the fairest thing in the world,
Embracing seven hills with a single wall.
And earlier still, before the Cretan king,
Dictaean Jove, held sway and an impious age
Of men began to feast on slaughtered oxen,
This life was led on earth by golden Saturn,   538
When none had ever heard the trumpet blown
Or heard the sword-blade clanking on the anvil.

But now we have traversed a course of many leagues:
High time to unyoke the steaming necks of our horses.

Book 3 deals, in two equal parts, with animals. The first, 1–283, is about horses and cattle, mostly in the context of breeding. The second, 284–566, introduced by a fresh proem of eleven lines, is about sheep and goats. Virgil is relying for information largely on Varro's Book 2, but unlike him has nothing on mules and donkeys, nothing on pigs and poultry, and dogs are given only a few lines (404–13). Nothing could make it clearer that the *Georgics* is a poem, not an exhaustive handbook. Horses, indeed, were little used on farms, where oxen did the main haulage. Virgil selected animals that suited his poetic book; and the horse in particular was intimately bound up with man. He would not want to clutter up his poem with miscellaneous and largely intractable detail. Horses were used for riding, racing and war, but for drawing carriages mules were generally preferred.

The metaphor for poetic activity of covering laps in a chariot which closes Book 2 provides a suitable transition to the proem of Book 3 (1–48; see pp. 25–6), with its similar metaphor from chariot-racing at Greek-style games. Virgil begins with deities of the country, Pales and Apollo, Italian and Greek, as patrons of this new song which, bypassing the fashionable themes from mythology, will win him poetic victory and fame. He returns to this motif at 40–45, but now with Maecenas named as patron, expressing his poetic exhilaration in a metaphor not from victory and racing in the games but from Bacchic revelry and hunting on the mountains. Three final lines pick up the promise to sing next of Caesar, foreshadowed in the temple to be erected to him. What ultimately emerged was the *Aeneid*.

The Pindaric proem prepares us for the first subject, the breeding of 'Olympic' racehorses, though from horses Virgil passes immediately to the brood cow (the bull is not dealt with here). She should be young, and her mating is spoken of in terms of human marriage. This extension leads to reflections on the transience of all life in the famous lines that so deeply moved Dr Johnson (66–8):

> Life's earliest years for wretched mortal creatures
> Are best, and fly most quickly: soon come on

> Diseases, suffering and gloomy age,
> Till Death's unpitying harshness carries them off.

Sex and death are to be dominant themes in this Book. A parallel passage of equal length on the breeding of horses follows (72–94). Selective as ever, Virgil deals here only with sires. He deliberately avoids the conscientious schematization of his chief source, Varro, preferring to contrast the clumsy, serviceable cow with the mettlesome thoroughbred horse, who is ennobled at the end by mythological comparison.

The theme of disease, age and death, given out at 67–8, is sounded more loudly at 95–100. But we are soon back with youth, and the points to look for in a colt. This gives occasion for a Homeric description of a chariot-race (103–12), and again there are ennobling allusions to mythology. Sires and dams are reunited in the section 123–56, which deals (somewhat confusedly as between horses and cattle) with preparation for their mating, and in the succeeding one (157–208) with the rearing of their young. The succinct directions are offset in the former by a vivid picture of the havoc that can be wrought by the gadfly (146–56), in the latter by a Homeric simile with the wind (196–201).

Mating leads up to the climax of the first part of the Book, a powerful passage (209–83) on precautions against frenzy brought on by sex. The famous passage 219–41, thoroughly anthropomorphic, on the contest of the two bulls who are rivals for a beautiful cow, is followed by one in which the theme is generalized to include all animals, the human animal being suddenly introduced at 258 in the person of Leander, subtly unnamed so that his highly individual story may yet suggest universal experience. It may be remarked that Virgil's attitude to sex reveals a nature more conscious of its dangers than its joys. He seems to see it as something that tends to degrade, debilitate and destroy, as we may sense in Eclogues 2, 8 and 10, in the stories in *Georgics* 4 of Aristaeus' offence and of the rending of Orpheus by sexually jealous women, and in the account in the *Aeneid* of the ruin of Dido. The sexlessness ascribed to the bees in Book 4 is presented as a matter for admiration.

The Romans bred cattle not only for draught but for sacrifice. The victim could be of either sex, but must be of unblemished appearance and well fattened. The sacrificed animal was eaten, but we do not hear much otherwise of rearing cattle for butcher's meat. There was a certain amount of sentiment involved. An old law forbidding it, perhaps of Pythagorean origin, is often mentioned. The idea that slaughtering of cattle for food was one of the symptoms of Iron Age degeneration occurs at *Georgics* 2.537. In any case the ox was in a special category, as the fellow-labourer with man. Apicius, in Book 8 of his cookery book, gives only three recipes for beef or veal, as against eleven for lamb or kid, thirteen for hare and seventeen for pig. Milking of cows for human consumption is mentioned only once in the *Georgics* (3.176–8), and there with a reservation. Goat's and sheep's milk was drunk.

The short proem to the second part of the Book echoes its predecessor, now in words recalling Lucretius, in its claim to high credit for poetic novelty. Sheep and goats must enlist all the poet's gifts if their treatment is to rise above banality. We are turning now from beasts that co-operate with man to ones that are passive and wholly dependent on his care. Virgil represents himself as going round his farm issuing orders. The goat was more important than it is to us, as the chief provider of milk, though its nibbling was notoriously damaging to saplings and shrubs. The passage ends with an idyll of summer (323–38), when in Italy the flocks can feed all day with only occasional guidance from the herdsmen. By contrast with this golden mean of climate we are given vignettes (339–83) of two extremes, the life of the nomad shepherds of North Africa and of the cattlemen of the frozen steppes, rhetorical elaborations of Hellenistic ethnography (the latter was drawn on by Ovid to portray the rigours of his place of exile on the Black Sea). A few lines about the production of wool and milk are succeeded by precautions against dangers (403–73) culminating in diseases and death (of which we have had forebodings); and so the tremendous finale, a description of the devastation caused by animal plague parallel to that of the devastation caused by lust which was the climax of the first part of the Book. It professes to recall a particular plague in the Alpine region north of the Adriatic, but its rhetorical impetus carries it beyond the sober bounds of probability. We now meet with the victorious racehorse and the useful ox of the first part in the hour of their undoing. Even after mass burials the infection survives in clothing to fasten on human beings. With a starkness more effective than any peroration could have been, the Book here breaks off. This finale matches that of Book 1, both contrasting with the eulogy of country life at the end of Book 2.

Lucretius (6.1138–286) had devoted 150 lines to a vivid description of the human plague at Athens in the time of Pericles, described for all time by Thucydides. In six lines he mentions the disappearance then of birds and wild animals, and the death of faithful dogs in the streets. This most probably gave Virgil his idea, and there are a number of symptoms in common; but in him the proportion is reversed because his subject involved him in dealing chiefly with animals. The sea animals, fishes and snakes are implausible as victims of the contagion, and his inclusion of human beings is questionable. It is easier to believe that he is culling gruesome symptoms from various sources and adding ones from his own fertile imagination. The fact that he introduces the Fury Tisiphone among the causes, and mythical healers as being baffled, is indication enough that the whole passage is to be read as literature, not as history or science.

Book 3

You too, great Pales, we will sing, and you
Famed keeper of flocks beside Amphrysus' stream
And, Pan's Arcadian woods and rivers, you.
Those other themes that might have served to charm
The idle mind are all so hackneyed now.
Who has not heard about the grim Eurystheus
Or those notorious altars of Busiris?
Who has not harped upon the youthful Hylas,
Latona's Delos or Hippodameia
And Pelops, charioteer conspicuous   7
For his ivory shoulder? I must find a way
Of my own to soar above the common ground
And 'fly victorious on the lips of men'.
   I will be first, if life is granted me,
To lead in triumph from Greek Helicon
To my native land the Muses. I will be first
To bring you, Mantua, Idumaean palms,
And in green meadows raise a marble temple
Beside the water where the Mincius,
Embroidering his banks with tender rushes,
In sweeping loops meanders.
In the middle of the shrine, as patron god,
I will have Caesar placed, and in his honour
Myself as victor in resplendent purple
Will drive a hundred chariots by the river.
For me all Greece, deserting the Alpheüs,
Olympia's river, and the groves of Nemea
In racing and in boxing will compete.
Myself as priest, my brow with olive-wreathed,
Will offer gifts. I see myself already   22
Leading the solemn procession joyfully
To the shrine and watching bullocks sacrificed,
Or in the theatre viewing the change of scenes
And Britons rising woven in crimson curtains.

[handwritten marginalia, left: "building a shrine"]

[handwritten marginalia, right: "construc. of temple as symbolic of construc. of a poem"] 15

On the temple doors I will have carved in gold
And solid ivory the hordes of Ganges
In battle and our Romulus' victory,
And here great Nile in flood, surging with war,
And columns rising decked with prows of bronze,
There Asian cities tamed, Niphates' heights   30
Conquered, the Parthian cunning in his flight
Shooting his arrows backward, and two trophies
Snatched from far separated enemies,
A double Triumph from two utmost shores.
Then Parian marbles, lifelike images,
Shall stand – the progeny of Assaracus,
Famed heroes of the Jove–descended race,
The patriarch Tros and Troy's originator,
Apollo. Wretched Envy shall be seen
Cowering before the Furies and Cocytus'   37
Merciless stream, Ixion's snaky bonds
And monstrous wheel, and the rock unmasterable.

　　Meanwhile however let my Muse pursue
The woods and glades of the Dryads, virgin country,
No soft assignment by your will, Maecenas.
You only spur my mind to high ambitions.
Up, then, and break the bonds of sluggishness!
Cithaeron calls me with its mighty clamour,
Taÿgetus' baying hounds and Epidaurus
Tamer of horses, and the roaring forests   45
Reverberate to reinforce the cry.
Yet soon I will gird myself to celebrate
The fiery fights of Caesar, make his name
Live in the future for as many years
As stretch from old Tithonus down to Caesar.

　　Whether a man breeds horses, coveting
Olympic palms, or sturdy steers for ploughing,
Let him look above all to the features of the dam.
The champion cow looks fierce, her head's uncouth,
Her neck thickset, her dewlaps pendulous   52

From jaw to legs, her flanks long as can be,
All on a big scale, even her feet. The ears
Under her crooked horns are shaggy. A hide
Brindled with white is not a disadvantage.
Impatience of the yoke, a tendency
To angry butting and a bull-like face
Are not amiss. She should be tall throughout
And sweep her tracks behind her with her tail.

    The age for lawful wedlock and for childbirth
Begins with four years, ceases with the tenth.   61
For the rest of her life she's neither fit for breeding
Nor strong enough for ploughing. Within those years
Cattle are young and lusty: loose the males
Among them, be the first to put your beasts
To mating, breed and breed again your stock.
Life's earliest years for wretched mortal creatures
Are best, and fly most quickly: soon come on
Diseases, suffering and gloomy age,
Till Death's unpitying harshness carries them off.
Dams there will always be with whose appearance   69
You are not satisfied; replace them always
Or you'll regret your loss; anticipate
And every year select new stock for breeding.

    With horses likewise you must use selection.
Be sure, with those you destine to bring up
As the hope of the stable, from their tenderest age
To take especial pains. From the very first
The thoroughbred young foal pacing the paddock
Lifts his feet higher, lowers them lissomly.
He leads the way in braving fearsome rivers
Or risking his safety on an untried bridge,   77
Nor shies at empty noise. His neck is high,
His head clean-cut, his barrel short, his back
Well-fleshed; his gallant chest ripples with muscle.
(For colour, bay and roan are fine, the worst
Are white and dun.) The thoroughbred, again,

At any distant sound of arms is restive,
[Ears pricking, limbs a-quiver; loudly snorting
His nostrils churn the pent-up fire within.
His mane is thick, and falls on his right shoulder   86
When tossed.]A double ridge runs down his back.
His hoof digs into the ground, its solid horn
Making a heavy thud.
Such Cyllarus was, whom Pollux of Amyclae
Broke in, and those made famous by Greek poets,
The pair of Mars and great Achilles' team.
Such too was Saturn himself, when swiftly flying
In the shape of a horse at the coming of his wife
He shook his streaming mane and as he fled
Filled Pelion's heights with his shrill whinnying.   94
   Yet even such, when burdened with disease
Or sluggish now with years he begins to fail,
You must shut indoors, repressing any pity
For pitiful old age. An ageing stallion
Is cool in passion, fruitlessly performs
A thankless task. And when it comes to battle,
Like fire in stubble impotently blazing,
His rage is null. So note especially
Mettle and years. Then look for other merits,
And pedigree: the grief of each in losing,   102
His pride in victory. Have you not seen
In a race how bursting from the barrier
The chariots charging headlong for the lead
Devour the track, while youthful hopes run high
Among the drivers, and their bounding hearts
Are drained with thrilling fear? Whirling their whips
And stooping to loose the reins, on, on they press,
Wheels heated with their speed. Now low, now high
They seem to rise uplifted from the ground
Clean through the air. No letting up, no respite.   110
A cloud of sand arises, and they feel
Damp on their backs the breath of their pursuers.
Such is their thirst for praise, their will to win.

Erichthonius was the first who dared to yoke
Four horses to a chariot and to race
Standing above the wheels to victory.
Riding on horses and manoeuvring
With bit and bridle were the Lapiths' gift;
They taught the arts of galloping fully armed
And proudly rounding paces. Either training   117
Is equally exacting, and for both
The trainers seek a young horse, spirited
And keen to race, even if they have in the stable
One who has often routed enemies
Or claims to have come from Epirus or Mycenae
Or to be sprung from Neptune's famous steed.

    With this in mind, as breeding-time draws near,
They set to work and take the greatest care
To fatten with firm flesh their chosen leader,
The destined lord of the herd. For him they cut   125
Flowering herbs, they ply him with fresh water
And corn, to make him no deficient master
Of his seductive task and let no leanness
Transmitted from the sire affect the young.
As for the dams, they keep them spare on purpose,
And when they observe by tell-tale signs the stirring
Of sexual desire, withhold their fodder
Of leaves and bar them from their drinking-places;
And often too they harass them with running
And sweat them in the sun; this at the season   132
When the threshing floor is groaning with pounded grain
And empty chaff flies in the freshening Zephyr.
Their object, that no pampering should cloy
The genital field nor clog and deaden its furrows,
But lust be thirstily snatched and stored within.

    Care for the sires now lessens, for the dams
In turn increases. When, their months come round,
They wander pregnant, let not anyone
Set cows in yoke to draw the heavy waggon,
Nor let the mares gallop along the highway,   141

Career across the fields at heady speed
Or swim in swirling torrents. In spacious glades
Men graze them, or beside a brimming river
Where banks are greenest, lush with moss and herbage,
Sheltered by caves and overhanging rocks.

    Among the groves of Silarus and the holmoaks
That clothe Alburnus swarms a breed of insect
The Romans call *asilus* but the Greeks
Oistros, the gadfly. Fierce it is, emitting
A vicious buzzing. Terrified by this   149
Whole herds break up stampeding through the woods;
The very air, the woods and Tanager's
Parched banks, are shattered and maddened by their bellows.
This is that monstrous pest devised by Juno
For dreadful vengeance on Inachian Io,
Turned to a cow. From this (for noonday heat
Intensifies its onslaught) you will spare
Your pregnant beasts by pasturing the herd
At dawn, or when the stars bring on the night.

    After their birth the calves in turn receive   157
All the attention. Straight away the herdsman
Must brand them with the markings of their stock,
Distinguishing those set aside for breeding,
Those kept for sacrifice, and those reserved
For breaking clods and cleaving shaggy ploughland.
The rest are sent to pasture in the meadows.
Those you will educate for farm employment
On special duties you must first encourage
In calfhood, and begin their discipline
While still their spirits are at the docile age.   165
First tie around their necks thin osier-nooses;
Then, when the freeborn necks are now accustomed
To servitude, still using those same nooses,
Link pairs of bullocks and make them march together.
Now let them often draw across the land
Unloaded wheels that barely print the dust;
Later a beechwood axle heavily laden

[margin note: "classes" of horses]

May strain and creak, the wheels behind the bullocks
Hitched to a brassbound pole. While they are young
And still unbroken you will gather for them   174
Not only grass and little willow-leaves
And marshy sedge, but tender hand-picked corn.
Nor will your cows, as in our fathers' day,
When newly calved fill pails with snowy milk,
But save their udders for their cherished offspring.
    But if your mind is bent on cavalry
For savage warfare or on wheels that speed
Beside the Alpheüs at Olympia
Where chariots race amid the trees of Jove,
Your horse must learn before all else to stomach   182
The sight of dashing arms and the trumpets' blare,
To endure the grind of groaning wheels, the jangling
Of harness in the stall; then more and more
To crave the coaxing praises of the trainer
And love the sound of patting on his neck.
These enterprises let the colt essay
As soon as weaned, still weak and trembling, still
Unused to life, and by degrees entrust
His mouth to gentle halters. Presently,
A three-year-old approaching his fourth summer,   190
Let him start to pace the ring, to tread the ground
With regular-sounding footsteps, and to trace
Alternate circles with his lissom legs,
A picture of application. Now he's ready
To challenge the winds to a race, and skimming over
The open plain, as if released from the reins,
Leave scarce a trace in the dust.
As when the North Wind from the Arctic shores
Gathers to swoop, deploying squalls before him
And dry clouds over the steppes; then standing corn   198
And watery tracts under the gentle gusts
Quiver, the treetops rustle, and the rollers
Drive shoreward. On he flies sweeping alike
Both land and sea beneath him.

A horse like that will either sweat to round
The course in Elis with its giant laps,
Mouth flecked with bloody foam, or better draw
The Belgic chariot with obedient neck.
Then only, when at last he's broken in,
Build up his frame with fortifying mash: 205
Unbroken horses fortified too soon
Will prove unmanageable, and when you catch them
Scorn to obey the lash and the hard bit.
    But no attention more conserves their strength
Than fending off the goads of blinding Venus,
Whether you care for cattle or for horses.
Therefore men banish bulls to lonely pastures
Far off, beyond some mountain barrier
Or broad expanse of river, or keep them closely
Confined with a well-filled manger. For a female   214
Slowly consumes their strength and burns it up
With sight of her, and will not let them think
Of woods or pasture, she with her fetching wiles;
And often she constrains her proud-horned lovers
To duel with one another. In Sila's forest
Grazes a lovely heifer. For her sake
The bulls contend, charging alternately
In violent battle. Many a wound is opened,
Dark blood streams down their sides, and horn to horn
They butt each other bellowing terribly,   222
Till woods and sky from end to end re-echo.
Nor do the rivals care to stall together.
The loser goes his way to unknown parts
Far off, an exile, groaning ceaselessly
For his disgrace and for the blows inflicted
By the arrogant victor, groaning equally
For love lost unavenged; with one last look
He quits his stable and ancestral kingdom.
Thereafter diligently he trains himself,
Lies on an unstrewn bed of hard rock   230
All night, with prickly rushes and coarse leafage

For fodder, tests himself, and learns to put
Fury into his horns, lungeing at tree-trunks,
Sparring with the air and kicking up the sand
In practice for the battle. Finally,
His forces mustered and his strength renewed,
He sallies out and charges at full tilt
Against his now forgetful enemy.
As when a wave begins far out to sea
To whiten, draws its billow from the deep,   238
And rolling to the shore roars on the rocks
To crash cliff-high. The eddies of the backwash
Toss up dark shingle from the water's depths.
  Indeed all species in the world, of men,
Wild beasts and fish, cattle and coloured birds
Rush madly into the furnace: love is common   — *sex drive*
To all. Only its seasonal heat can drive
The lioness, unmindful of her cubs,
Fiercely to prowl abroad, or rouse again
Lumbering bears to spread throughout the forest   247
Havoc and death. Then is the boar most fierce,
The tigress at her worst. No time is that
For wandering in the lonely Libyan desert.
Look how the stallion quivers in every limb
If once that well-known scent comes down the wind.
Then neither man-made bridle or harshest whip
Nor rocks or precipices can restrain him,
Nor intervening rivers strong enough
To uproot and whirl whole mountains in their flood.
Even the Sabine boar goes hurtling by.   255
He whets his tusks, digs at the ground before him
And rubs each flank on a tree to make it hard,
Proof against any wound. What of the youth
Inflamed to the very bone by cruel love?
Think of one swimming late in the black of night
Across a strait lashed with the burst of storms.
Above him thunders the vast gate of heaven,
And round him waves dashing on rocks resound.

No pleas of wretched parents can call him back,
Nor any thought for the girl he's dooming to death.   263
Think of the spotted lynxes, Bacchus' team,
The savage breeds of wolf and dog, the duels
That peaceful stags fight in their rutting season.
But surely mares above all display this madness:
Venus herself possessed them on the day
At Potniae when his chariot-team devoured
The limbs of Glaucus. Over Gargarus
And the roaring flood of Ascanius love leads them;
They conquer mountain steeps and swim through rivers.
Soon as the flame of lust catches their vitals   271
(In spring, most like, for warmth returns in spring
Into their bones), they take their stand together
On a high cliff, all turned towards the Zephyr
To snuff its gentle breezes; so that often
With no preceding wedlock they conceive,
Miraculously pregnant by the wind.
Then over rocks and crags and lowland valleys
They scatter, not towards the East Wind and sunrise
But towards the North, North-West, or where the South,
Darkest of winds, rises to chill the sky   279
With watery mourning. Then and only then
Hippomanes, as shepherds aptly call it,
'Horse-madness', oozes slowly from their groin,
Which often cruel stepmothers collect
To mix with herbs and evil incantations.

   But time is flying, flying beyond recall,
While captivated I linger lovingly,
Touring from this to that. Enough of herds:
My second part remains, to drive afield
My flocks of fleecy sheep and shaggy goats.   287
Here's work for you, stalwart farmers, and here's hope
Of earning praise. I'm well aware how great
A task it is by mastery of words
To invest such humble things with dignity;

Book 3

But love transports me to Parnassus' steeps;
I tread with rapture heights from which no track
Beaten by others winds with gentle slope
Down to Castalia's spring. Now, gracious Pales,
Inspire me now to sing in lofty tones.

First I decree that sheep should crop their fodder   295
In folds well littered till the near approach
Of leafy summer. Strew the hardened ground
Beneath with straw and fern in generous armfuls,
Otherwise frost may harm the tender flock,
Infesting it with scab and nasty foot-rot.
Then, passing on, I advise you give your goats
Plenty of arbute leaves and running water;
And make their stalls face south, out of the wind,
To catch the midday sun in winter-time,
When chilly Aquarius, setting in February,   304
Waters the skirts of the departing year.
These too need no less care, nor will our profit
Be less, though fleeces from Miletus, dyed
In Tyrian purple, fetch a handsome price.
Goats have more offspring, goats produce a wealth
Of milk: the more the foaming pail receives,
From udders drained, the richer flows the stream
When next the teats are pressed. To add to this,
The herdsman clips the beard from the hoary chin
And shears the shaggy coat of the Libyan he-goat   312
For army use and sailcloth for poor sailors.
They browse in woods and in Arcadian highlands,
On prickly briars and thorns that love the steep,
And of their own accord, leading their kids,
Return at nightfall punctually to stall,
Brushing the threshold with their swollen udders.
So all the more because they less demand
Of human care you'll shield them from the frost
And icy winds and bring them cheerfully
Branches for fodder and keep your hayloft open   321

All through the winter-time.
   But when glad summer at the Zephyrs' call
Sends sheep and goats alike to glades and meadows,
Let us hasten as the morning star appears
To the cool pastures, while the day is young,
The grass is gleaming, and on the tender blades
There still is dew delightful to the herd.
Then, when the sky's fourth hour has brought their thirst
To a head, and with incessant dinning drone
Cicalas burst the bushes, I will lead   328
The flocks to drink at wells or standing pools
Water that runs in troughs of ilex-wood.
But in the noonday heat I'll have them seek
A shady valley where some ancient oak
Of Jupiter with venerable trunk
Extends huge branches, or an ilex-grove
Thick-planted broods with dark and holy shadow;
Then feed again till the sun sets and drink
Clear water when the evening star is cooling
The air and the moon refreshing the glades with dew,   337
And calls of birds re-echo, from the shore
The kingfisher's, the warbler's from the thorn.
   Need I pursue the theme of Libyan shepherds,
Their pastures, scattered huts and settlements?
Often their flock will graze both night and day
A whole month through, and pass beyond all shelter
Far out into the endless desert plains.
The African herdsman takes along with him
All his possessions – house and home and arms,
His Cretan quiver and his Spartan dog;   345
Just like a Roman soldier valiantly
Making a forced march under his cruel pack
Of legionary equipment to surprise
The enemy, camp pitched, in line of battle.
   Contrast the scene among the Scythian tribes
Beside the Sea of Azov or the Danube
That rolls a tide turbid with yellow sand,

Or where Mount Rhodope arches her back
Right up to the central pole. There herds are kept
Shut up in stalls; no grass is seen on the plain,   353
No leaf upon the tree, but far and wide
The land lies shapeless under drifts of snow
And piles of ice full seven cubits high.
Winter is endless there, and nor'-west winds
Whistle with endless cold; nor does the sun
Ever disperse the pall of pallid fog
Either in driving his chariot up the sky
Or plunging it into the crimson ocean.
In running rivers sudden sheets of ice
Congeal, until the water's back can bear   361
Iron-bound wheels, and that which recently
Welcomed light craft now welcomes lumbering waggons.
Bronze vessels burst quite often, clothing freezes
On the body, an axe is used to serve the wine,
Whole ponds are found turned into solid ice
And uncombed beards bristle with icicles.
Meanwhile the air is no less thick with snow;
Beasts perish, frozen stiff huge shapes of oxen
Stand starkly round, and huddling herds of deer
Lurk paralysed beneath fresh drifts of snow,   370
Their antlers barely showing. Hunters need
No hounds to unleash against them, nets to trap them
Or scaring crimson feathers to stampede them,
But as they push against the mountainous mass
In vain, the men attack them steel in hand,
Butcher their bellowing victims ruthlessly
And bear them off in noisy triumph home.
Themselves, they live at ease deep underground,
Secure in dugouts, warmed by logs they pile,
Even whole elms, at the hearth and give to the flames.   378
The night they spend in games, and cheerfully
Brew serviceberry ale to do for wine.
Wild tribesmen these who exist in the far north
Under the Bear, battered by mountain-winds,

Their bodies clothed in tawny pelts of beasts.

If wool is your concern, then first of all
Banish the prickly growth of burrs and caltrops;
Avoid rich pastures; and from the very start
Select whole flocks with fleeces soft and white.
As for the ram, though dazzling white he be,   387
If but the tongue beneath the slimy palate
Is black, for fear the fleeces of your lambs
Bear dusky spots, reject him: look around,
There's ample room for choice.
By such a gift, Moon-goddess, of snow-white wool
Pan, god of Arcady, lured and beguiled you,
Summoning you to the depths of a wood; and you
Did not disdain his summons.
But he who cares for milk must pluck and bring
With his own hand plenty of shrub-trefoil   394
And lotus and salted herbage to the stalls.
Salt gives the goats more appetite for drink;
Their udders swell the more, and in their milk
There lurks a salty flavour. Many keep
Kids from their dams as soon as they are born,
Fitting their noses' tips with iron muzzles.
The milk men draw at dawn and through the day
They cheese at night, and what they draw at nightfall
They send away by dawn in wickered jars
(The shepherd goes to town), or lightly salt it   402
And store it up for use in winter-time.

And do not underrate the care of dogs:
Brisk Spartan pups and keen Molossian hounds,
Feed both on fattening whey. With them on guard
No need to fear thieves in the stalls at night,
Or wolves' attacks, or stealing up behind you
Iberian bandits. Often too with hounds
You'll chase the shy wild asses, course the hare,
Or hunt the doe with hounds. Often you'll drive

Wild boars ejected from their forest wallows   411
By a baying pack, or over mountain heights
Force a huge stag with clamour into the nets.

   Back to your stalls. Burn fragrant cedar there
And oust with fumes of gum the vicious snakes.
Often beneath neglected pens there lurks
A dangerous viper, shrinking from the daylight,
Or an adder, curse of cattle, such as love
To creep into the shelter of dark buildings
And stab the herd with poison, is nestling there.
Quick, herdsman, pick up a stone, pick up a stick,   420
And as he rears his swelling, hissing throat
To threaten, down with him! See, he's bolted now
And hidden his frightened head deep underground;
His central coils and the end of his writhing tail
Are slackening and he's trailing his last slow curves.
Then there's that terror of Calabria's glades,
A snake that rears its tortuous scaly back
And length of belly mottled with huge blotches.
So long as streams are gushing from their sources,
So long as south winds bringing rain in spring   429
Keep the land moist, it lodges in river banks
Or lurks in pools to glut its cavernous maw
Unconscionably with fish and chattering frogs;
But when the marsh dries up and the earth gapes
With the sun, it darts off into the parched land,
Where, rolling its blazing eyes, maddened with thirst
And terrified by the heat, it rages abroad.
Far be it from me to indulge in a nap
Under the open sky, or lie outstretched
On the grass of a wooded hillside, at the time   436
When, fresh from casting his slough, gleaming with youth,
He glides along, leaving at home his young
Or eggs maybe, and towers towards the sun
Flickering out of his mouth that three-forked tongue.

Diseases too, their causes and their symptoms,
I will expound. Foul scab attacks the sheep
When chilly rain and winter's bristling hoar-frost
Have seeped right down to the quick, or unwashed sweat
Has clung to the newly-shorn, or prickly briars
Have torn their flesh. For this the shepherds dip   445
The whole flock in fresh streams. The ram is plunged
Into the race and launched with sodden fleece
For the current to carry along. Or after shearing
They smear the skin with bitter olive-lees,
And mix fresh sulphur, scum of silver, pitch
From Ida, softened wax, strong hellebore
And squills and black bitumen. But no treatment
Relieves these troubles more effectively
Than if you have the heart to take a knife
And lance the ulcer's head: the mischief lives   453
And thrives upon concealment, while the shepherd
Sits praying the gods for signs of better luck.
Further, if raging pain has penetrated
To the joints of the bleating beasts and parching fever
Consumes their limbs, it helps to draw away
The fiery heat by cutting through the vein
That throbs with blood in the middle of the hoof,
As the Bisaltae and Gelonians do,
Wild nomads in the mountain fastnesses
Of Rhodope and the Getic wilderness,   462
To curdle with horse's blood the milk they drink.
If you see a sheep inclined to wander off
And seek relieving shade, or listlessly
Nibble the top of the grass, or lag behind,
Or sink in the act of feeding in midfield,
Or when night falls return late and alone,
Quell the offence immediately by slaughter
Before the terrible contagion spreads
Unmarked to all and sundry. Thicker than squalls
Swept by a hurricane from off the sea   470
Plagues sweep through livestock; and not one by one

Diseases pick them off, but at a stroke
A summer's fold, present and future hopes,
The whole stock, root and branch. For proof of this
Look at the lofty Alps and Noric hilltowns
And the fields beside Illyrian Timavus
Now, so long afterwards – the shepherds' kingdom
Deserted, far and wide the valleys empty.
    For there it was that once a woeful season
Of tainted atmosphere and plague arose,   **478**
Torrid with all the furnace-heat of autumn.
All manner of creatures, tame and wild, it killed,
Infecting pools, contaminating fodder.
The road to death was crooked: first of all
A fiery thirst coursing through all their veins
Shrivelled their wretched limbs, then fluid in turn
Welled up, absorbing piecemeal all their bones
Rotted with the disease. Often a victim
In the very course of worship of the gods,
Standing before the altar while the fillet,   **486**
The snow-white wreath, was bound about its head,
Fell dead amid the dawdling acolytes;
Or if the priest had struck the blow in time,
The yield of entrails placed upon the altar
Failed to blaze up; nor could the seer supply
Interpretation; the knife that slit the throat
Showed scarce a drop of blood, and a meagre trickle
Darkened no more than the surface of the sand.
Then calves in the fields, amid abundant grass,
Are dying on all sides, or by full mangers   **494**
Gasping away their last sweet breath of life.
Mild dogs go raving mad. A racking cough
Shakes the sick pigs and chokes their swollen gullets.
The once victorious racehorse sinks, his keenness
Wilting, forgets to feed, refuses drink.
He paws the ground incessantly; his ears
Droop, and a fitful sweat breaks out around them,
The chilly sweat of death; his skin is dry,

Hard to the touch, insensible to stroking.
These are the early signs of death's approach.   503
But as the worsening sickness takes its course
His eyes become inflamed, his breath deep-drawn,
Laden at times with groans; and bouts of sobbing
Shudder throughout his flanks; a gush of blood
Comes from his nostrils and his roughened tongue
Chokes his blockaded throat. Relief was sought
By pouring wine through an inserted horn.
That seemed the only hope of cure; but soon
(God blind the wicked so, but spare the just!)
This in itself proved fatal: stimulated,   511
They blazed with frenzy and, though sick to death,
Tore at their bodies with their own bare teeth.

   Look at that bull! Steaming under the strain
Of the plough he crashes, vomiting blood and foam,
And utters a last groan. Sadly the ploughman
Goes to unyoke the mate that mourns his brother
And leaves the plough stuck there, its work unfinished.
No shade of lofty trees, no luscious meadows
Can cheer that beast again, nor any stream
Clearer than amber gliding over stones   522
Down to the plain: his flanks collapse unstrung,
Dullness benumbs his listless eyes, his neck
Droops with its nodding weight and sinks to the ground.
What good can his loyal service do him now
And all that heavy ploughing? Yet immune
From Bacchus' gifts of Massic and immune
From harmful feasts when course is heaped on course
Oxen have leaves for fare and simple grass,
The health they drink is drawn from racing brooks,
Pure water, nor do cares disturb their slumbers.   530

   They say that in that region then alone
Could heifers not be found for sacrifice
To Juno, and to her high treasury
The car was drawn by buffaloes ill-matched.
It was left for men to scratch the earth with mattocks,

Scrape with their nails for planting, and pull waggons
Creaking o'er hill and dale with straining shoulders.
The wolf at night scouts for no place of ambush
Around the fold nor prowls about the flocks:
A sharper pang has tamed him. Timid does   539
And stags once shy now stray among the hounds
And wander round the buildings. Now the tide
Strands on the edge of the shore, like shipwrecked corpses,
The brood of the boundless sea and every species
Of swimming creature. Seals in panic flight
Take to the rivers. Vainly the viper seeks
Security in the windings of her lair:
She, with the startled watersnake, whose scales
Bristle with terror, dies. The very birds
Find in the air no favour: even they   546
Plunge headlong, leaving life beneath the clouds.
Changes of pasture now gave no relief.
New treatments made things worse; renowned physicians –
Chiron the son of Phillyra, Melampus
The son of Amythaon – owned defeat.
Let loose from Stygian darkness into daylight
Tisiphonê the ghastly Fury raged
Driving before her Terror and Disease,
And daily higher reared her hungry head.
With bleating of flocks and constant lowing of cattle   554
The dried-up riverbanks and sloping hillsides
Echoed. And now the Fury dealt out death
In droves, and even in the very stalls
Piled up the foully rotting carcases
Until men learned to bury them in pits
Since hides were no more use and nobody
Could cleanse the flesh with water or reclaim it
With fire. They could not even shear the fleeces,
So eaten up were these with sores and filth,
Nor touch the rotting web. If any tried   563
To don the loathsome clothing, feverish blisters
And filthy sweat ran down his stinking limbs.

disease could spread to humans

He had not long to wait: the accursèd fire
Would soon be preying on his infected body.

Introduction to Book 4

Book 4 is about bees. Virgil selected them from among farmyard stock for treatment partly, perhaps, because of the importance of honey as the only sweetener in antiquity, but chiefly, no doubt, because they lent themselves admirably to his poetic purposes, with the opportunities they provide not only for social and moral nuances, but also for picturesque description, anthropomorphic sympathy and humorous irony, and for the peculiar interest of their natural history. But the latter part of the Book, from line 315, is entirely different, a superb poetic climax, the story of Aristaeus. This is discussed separately here because its connection with the rest of the poem is controversial.

Virgil had at his disposal a number of treatises on bees dating back at least to Aristotle, including one in verse by Nicander, but little survives from these. If there seem to be more erroneous ideas in this part of the work than elsewhere (see notes), that is due to the particular difficulty of studying bees without a glass observation hive (though Aristotle is said to have had one of transparent horn) and without a microscope. It was not until the seventeenth century that even some important areas of their nature began to be understood. It was also particularly tempting to explain their motives and conduct in human terms.

There is only a short proem (1–7), as happy and healthy after the catastrophic plague at the end of Book 3 as the short proem to Book 2 is after the miserable chaos of civil war at the end of Book 1. An amusingly mock-heroic tone is set:

> Gallant commanders and the institutions
> Of a whole nation, its characters, pursuits,
> Communities and warfare.

'The play of great and small' (Klingner) is a feature of the early part of the Book.

Lines 8–115 deal with the siting and construction of the hive. The description (51–66) of the surroundings to be sought is idyllic. Nature is no longer working against man's efforts: for the most part man has only to co-operate with the bees' creative instincts. Or if they err, he can easily correct them. Lines 65–85 contain a vivid (and wholly imaginary) description, in epic military terms, of a battle between the armies of rival leaders. The pay-off lines 86-7 both reduce the bees to size (man is firmly in control) and give man himself a timely reminder of the futility of his own wars (subordinate in their turn, the hint is, to the control of Jupiter):

> These ardent passions and these prodigious contests
> A little handful of dust will lay to rest.

There is also, perhaps, an oblique reminder that we ourselves are 'proud and angry dust' – *pulvis et umbra sumus*.

Lines 88–102 tell how to deal with the rival leaders: you must ruthlessly kill off the inferior and foster the followers of the superior. When we recollect that Virgil was finishing the *Georgics* in the months that saw the defeat of Antony by Caesar and recall his subsequent characterization of their two hosts in the prophetic engravings on the shield given by Venus to Aeneas at *Aeneid* 8.617–88, we can hardly help seeing this battle of the bees as a contemporary allegory. Yet four lines later he is saying that, if the swarm shows signs of flightiness, you can easily restrain it by tearing off the leaders' wings. Caesar's wings too? We have been warned not to press suggestiveness into downright allegory. The military motif emerges again at 108: 'strike camp and move the standards.' And finally the Hard Work theme, dominant in Book 1, is heard again, with 'himself' thrice repeated of the efforts demanded of the good beekeeper in securing suitable plants to rear in the neighbourhood of the hive.

Hitherto Virgil has been dealing with the natural history of bees for its own sake. He now requires a break, and takes this passage as cue for an interlude, the sketch of a fifth Georgic on gardens which he cannot develop, he says, because time is pressing (presumably because he has committed himself now to epic): his ship is nearing port – the Seafaring Theme again. The sketch (116–48) takes the form of the description of a garden he once saw near Tarentum, made out of nothing by an old Cilician settler.

The break was needed because he was now turning to a different aspect of the bees, introduced by a mythological allusion. Bees have *mores*, he alleges, unique in the animal kingdom, given them by Jupiter as a *reward*: communism, even of children, loyalty to home, laws and leaders, provision for the future, pooling of gains and division of labour. Finally, in a class by themselves, they are non-sexual. Since these *mores* are spoken of as a reward, we must assume that Virgil thinks them advantageous, though he might not wish them to be adopted *in toto* by contemporary Romans. Co-operation for the common good and chastity were correctives desperately needed by the society described in the finale of Book 1 and, by way of contrast with country life, in that of Book 2. They presage, indeed, the Augustan programme of moral reform (see p. 26).

The passage 197–202, based on one ancient hypothesis, that young bees were gathered from flowers, not produced by copulation, is the obverse of 3.242–83, on the ubiquitous and destructive power of sexual lust (see p. 96). It merges into a general approbation of the bees' self-sacrifice for the common good, which ensures the abiding prosperity of the race, and to save their leader, which inevitably suggests Caesar and the prayer at the end of Book 1. This leads to a climax, the belief held by some that bees have a special portion of the divine spirit which, they say, pervades the whole creation (see p. 29).

At 228 we return to beekeeping without overtones, with honey-harvesting and the necessity, at all costs, of keeping the hive clean. By a natural transition from this we come to pests and diseases and how to remedy them; and so to the possibility of the extinction of a whole stock, and how to remedy that. Virgil recommends a procedure he attributes to the Egyptians in particular, the so-called *Bugonia*, spontaneous generation from the carcase of an ox, recommended indeed by many previous authorities, with the significant exception of Aristotle, without any experimental evidence. With the invention of this he credits 'the Arcadian master', Aristaeus.

The rest of the poem is in the form of a short epic of a kind fashionable at Rome in Virgil's day as part of the literary legacy of Alexandria (e.g. Catullus' *Peleus and Thetis*). It consists of a narrative, in this case that of Aristaeus' loss of his bees by disease and their replacement, with another narrative, directly or obliquely relevant, inset (in Catullus, Ariadne's desertion by Theseus and redemption by Bacchus; here, Orpheus' loss and abortive recovery of Eurydice). It is also Alexandrian in being an *aition*, a poem explaining the origin of a custom. The change from didactic is very abrupt, and the fourth-century commentator Servius knew of a story, mentioned by no one else, that a major change was made in the latter part of the Book: that originally it contained a eulogy of Virgil's great friend, the pioneer of subjective love-elegy as a *genre* and first Prefect of Egypt, Cornelius Gallus (see Eclogues 6 and 10); but that after his disgrace and suicide in 27 there was a substitution. In his note on Eclogue 10.1 he says that the whole of the second half of the Book was replaced by the story of Aristaeus (but it is hard to believe that Gallus could have had such a lion's share of praise in a public poem composed in Caesar Octavian's Italy and dedicated to Maecenas, both his superiors). But he is so vague that on *Georgics* 4.1 he only says that the Orpheus story was a substitute (but that is integral to the Aristaeus story, since the sacrifice that produced *Bugonia* requires motivation). Although some leading scholars had expressed scepticism, until about 1933 Servius' uncorroborated allegation held the field, and it still has some notable adherents[1]; but it was severely criticized independently by E. Norden and W. B. Anderson, and it is now generally discredited. The episode has therefore been treated as belonging to the original poem in the General Introduction (pp. 39–42).

Aristaeus was the son of Apollo and the nymph Cyrene, destined for immortality after a life on earth. Having lost all his bees he went to complain to his mother. She told him he must find out the cause from the clairvoyant sea-deity Proteus (315–414). Proteus, when finally constrained to answer, revealed that the Dryad Eurydice, wife of the minstrel Orpheus, had died of a snakebite incurred while fleeing from Aristaeus' amorous pursuit. It was her companion nymphs who in anger had punished him with the loss of his bees; and he went on to tell the story (actually irrelevant to the plot though not to the effect of the poem) of how Orpheus sought Eurydice in the Underworld, regained her, and then lost her finally, and how he was torn to pieces by jealous Thracian Bacchants for his single-minded devotion to her memory (453–527). Cyrene, who has been listening near by, now knows who must be propitiated. She instructs her son in the method of sacrifice appropriate to this, and, lo and behold, new bees are spontaneous-

---

1. e.g. K. Büchner, E. de Saint-Denis, W. Richter. For fuller discussion of the problem see L. P. Wilkinson, *The Georgics of Virgil* (1969), chapter V and appendix IV.

ly generated from the carcases by what is known as *Bugonia* (530–57).

The eight-line epilogue to the poem has been dealt with in the General Introduction (p. 24).

The heavenly gift of honey from the air
Is next my theme. Look kindly on this too,
Maecenas. I will show you a spectacle
To marvel at, a world in miniature,
Gallant commanders and the institutions
Of a whole nation, its character, pursuits,
Communities and warfare. Little the scale
To work on, yet not little is the glory
If unpropitious spirits do not cramp
A poet and Apollo hears his prayer.   7

   A site must first be chosen for your bees,
Fixed quarters, unexposed to winds (for wind
Prohibits them from bringing home their food),
Where there are neither sheep nor frisky kids
To trample down the flowers, nor blundering heifer
To dash the dew and bruise the springing grass.
Let not the spangled lizard's scaly back
Be seen in their rich dwelling, nor such birds
As bee-eaters and the fabled swallow Procne,
Her breast still reddened by her bloody hands;   15
For these spread havoc, snatching on the wing
The bees themselves to bear them in their beaks
As tit-bits for their cruelly gaping nestlings.
But let clear springs and moss-green pools be near
And hurrying through the grass a shallow stream,
A palm to shade their porch or a huge wild-olive.
Thus, when new kings lead out the earliest swarms
To claim their springtime and released from the cells
The young ones sport, a neighbouring bank may tempt them
To shelter from the heat, and in their path   22
A tree detain them with a leafy welcome.
Whether your water is a pond or stream,
Into the middle throw some willow branches

Athwart, and hefty stones, to give the bees
Plenty of landing-stages where they may
Alight and spread their wings to the summer sun
If ever an east wind has swooped to spray
Loiterers or to duck them in the deep.
And all around let green spurge-laurel bloom
With thyme that smells afar and with a wealth   31
Of pungent savory, and violet-beds
To drink the trickling stream.
    The hives themselves, whether you like them stitched
Of hollow cork or woven of pliant osiers,
Must have their entrance narrow: winter's grip
Solidifies the honey; summer's heat
Dissolves it into liquid. For the bees
Either extreme is harmful. Not for nothing
They strive to seal with wax each tiny crack
In the roof, and cram the entrances with paste   39
From flowers, and for this very purpose keep
The glue they have collected, stickier
Than birdlime or than pitch from Phrygian Ida.
And often, if the tale be true, they make
Snug, sheltered homes by tunnelling underground:
And deep in porous rock they may be found
Or holed in a rotten tree. But you yourself
Should plaster with smooth clay to keep them snug
Those chinky dormitories, and apply
A coat of leaves to finish. Let no yew   46
Be found too near the hive. Let no red crab
Be roasted on your hearth. Avoid a bog
Or place of stinking slime, or where the voice
Rebounds in hollow echo from the rocks.

    Now when the golden sun has driven winter
In rout beneath the earth and freed the sky
With summery light, the bees incontinently
Roam over glades and woodlands harvesting
Bright blooms, and lightly sip the river's surface.

Inspired by this with some mysterious joy   55
They tend their nests and young; inspired by this
They forge new wax and fashion sticky honey.
And so, when looking up you see the column
New issued from the hive swim heavenward
Through the liquid air of summer, and admire
How the dark cloud goes trailing down the wind,
Observe: they make a beeline for fresh water
Always, and leafy shelter. In such a spot
Scatter the scents appointed, pounded balm
And the humble honeywort; and raise a noise   64
Of tinkling all around, and shake the cymbals
Of the Mighty Mother. Of their own accord
They'll settle in the fragrant quarters, bury
Themselves instinctively in the inmost chambers.

    But maybe they have issued out for battle;
For often civil war between two kings
Irrupts with great commotion, and at once
You can presage mob violence arising
And hearts agog for war. A brassy, blaring
Reveille chides the laggards, and a sound   71
Is heard as of the bugle's broken bray.
Then bustling they assemble; wings are flashed,
Stings sharpened upon beaks and muscles tensed;
And round their king, right up to the royal tent,
They mass, and loudly challenge the enemy.
So, when a fine spring day and an open field
Are offered, out they sally; battle is joined;
High in the air a hum is heard; they merge
And mingle gathered into one huge ball,
Then tumble headlong, thick as hail from heaven   80
Or rain of acorns from a shaken oak.
The monarchs move amid the ranks of war
Conspicuous by the flashes on their wings,   → medals
Heroic hearts beating in tiny breasts,
Still steadfast not to yield till victory
Has driven these or those to turn in flight.

These ardent passions and these prodigious contests
A little handful of dust will lay to rest.
　　But when you have recalled from the field of battle
Both captains, single out the inferior　　　　　　　　　　　**89**
And put him to death, for fear his wasteful presence
Obstruct the work, and leave the palace free
For the better one to rule. There are two breeds:
The one will be aglow with golden markings
Of mail – the better one – conspicuous
In countenance and sheen of blazing scales,
The other unkempt with sloth, ingloriously
Trailing a bloated paunch. As are the aspects
Of the respective kings, so you will find
The bodies of their subjects; some of these　　　　　　　　**95**
Are filthy and unkempt, as a traveller
Who coming parched from a journey through thick dust
Spits out the dirt; but others gleam and flash,
Splendid in golden-spotted uniforms.
This is the sturdier breed, this in due season
Will yield you sweeter honey to extract,
And that not only sweet but clear as well
And fit to tame the harshness of your wine.
　　But if the swarm is aimless, gadding about
In the air, disdainful of the cells and leaving　　　　　　**104**
Its quarters to get cold, you must intervene
To check their giddy spirits from idle play.
To check them is no great task: just take the kings
And tear their wings off. While these stay at home
No one will dare to take off into the air,
Strike camp and move the standards. Let there be
Gardens to tempt them, breathing saffron flowers,
And, stationed with willow sickle to scare off thieves
And birds, Priapus of the Hellespont.
The beekeeper must go himself to fetch　　　　　　　　　　**112**
Thyme from the mountain heights and laurestines
For growing round the hive, himself must harden
His hands with rugged work, himself must plant

Vigorous slips and water them lovingly.

Indeed, were I not furling now my sails
In sight of the end of my task and hastening
To turn my prow to land, I would perhaps
Sing of the pride that careful husbandry
Can give to fertile gardens, of the rosebeds
That bloom at Paestum twice a year, and how   119
The endive revels in the brook it drinks,
Green banks delight in parsley, and the gourd
Twists through the grass to swell into a paunch;
Narcissus the late-flowering would be sung,
The curly acanthus' stem, the pallid ivy
And seashore-loving myrtle.
I well remember how, beneath the towers
Of old Tarentum where the dark Galaesus
Waters the yellow crops, I saw a man,
An old Cilician, who occupied   127
An acre or two of land that no one wanted,
A patch not worth the ploughing, unrewarding
For flocks, unfit for vineyards; he however
By planting here and there among the scrub
Cabbages or white lilies and verbena
And flimsy poppies, fancied himself a king
In wealth, and coming home late in the evening
Loaded his board with unbought delicacies.
He was the first in spring to gather roses,
In autumn, to pick apples; and when winter   134
Was gloomily still cracking rocks with cold
And choking streams with ice, he was already
Shearing the locks of the tender hyacinth
While grumbling at the lateness of the summer
And absence of west winds. And his again
Were the first bees to breed, the first to swarm
Abundantly and have their foaming honey
Squeezed from the combs. Plenty of limes he had
And laurestines; and all the fruit a tree

Promised in blossom-time's array to bear   143
It bore matured in autumn. Elms well-grown,
Pear-trees already hardened, even blackthorns
Already bearing sloes and planes already
Providing welcome shade for drinking parties
He planted out in rows successfully –
But I, restricted by my boundaries,
Must leave this theme to later generations.

   Now listen while I indicate the natures
Which Jove himself bestowed on bees, rewarding
Their service when, drawn by the tuneful sounds   150
Of the Curētĕs and their clashing bronzes,
They fed in Dictē's cave the King of Heaven.
Alone they hold their progeny in common,
Alone they share the housing of their city,
Passing their lives under exalted laws,
Alone they recognize a fatherland
And the sanctity of a home, and provident
For coming winter set to work in summer
And store their produce for the common good.
For some attend to victuals, covenanting   158
To labour in the field; some stay at home
And in its confines lay the first foundations
Of the combs with daffodil tears for propolis
And sticky glue from tree-bark, then suspend
The clinging wax; others initiate
The adolescent hopefuls of the tribe;
Some pack the purest honey and distend
The cells with liquid nectar; some by lot
Obtain the post of sentries at the gates
To take their turn at watching for rain or clouds   166
Or taking in the loads from foragers,
Or, falling in for action, drive the drones,
That pack of shirkers, from the common fold.
The workshop hums, and the honey reeks of thyme.
As when the Cyclopses forge thunderbolts

Deftly of ductile metal, some of them
Pump air from bullhide bellows, others plunge
The hissing bronze in troughs, while Etna groans
Under the weight of anvils. Mightily
They raise their arms in alternating rhythm   174
And turn the metal with their gripping tongs.
Just so (if small may be compared with great)
Innate acquisitiveness impels the bees
To ply their several tasks. The aged ones
Are town surveyors charged with building cells
And framing intricate houses, while the younger
Drag themselves home exhausted late at night,
Their thighs laden with thyme; for far and wide
They feed on arbutus, on pale green willow,
On garland flower and yellow crocuses   182
And sticky lime and dusky asphodel.
All toil together and all rest together.
At dawn they pour from the gates – no loitering –
Likewise when finally the evening star
Warns them to quit their pasture in the fields,
Then they make homeward, then they rest their bodies.
A hum is heard of gossiping on doorsteps.
At last, when all are tucked in bed, a silence
Falls for the night, and over their tired limbs
A well-earned slumber steals.   190
But when there's rain impending they do not range
So far from the stalls, nor will they trust the weather
When winds from the east are rising, but keep safe
Under their city walls and only venture
Brief sorties to get water or tiny pebbles
With which, as boats in a tossing sea take ballast,
They balance themselves in the unsubstantial clouds.
    Another custom that the bees approve
Will make you marvel: they forbear to indulge
In copulation or to enervate   198
Their bodies in Venus' ways, nor do they bear
Their young in travail, but themselves, unmated,

Gather their children in their mouths from leaves
And fragrant herbs, themselves supply their king
And infant citizens, and recreate
Their halls and waxen kingdoms. Often too
Wandering amid rough rocks they bruise their wings
And sacrifice their lives beneath their burdens,
Such is their love of flowers and such their pride
In generating honey. Thus it is   205
That though a narrow span of life awaits
Each individual (for none of them
Outlive their seventh summer) yet the stock
Remains immortal, and for many years
The house survives in fortune, and its annals
Count generation upon generation.

   Moreover neither Egypt nor the realm
Of Lydia, nor the Parthian populations,
Nor Median Hydaspes so regard
Their king. So long as the bees' king is safe   212
They all are of one mind. If he be lost,
Forthwith they break their loyalty, themselves
Plunder their edifice of treasured honey
And wreck the trellised cells. He is the guardian
Of all their works, him they admire, surround him
In cheering crowds and flock to form his escort,
Carry him shoulder-high, expose their bodies
In battle to protect him, and there seek
Through wounds a death with glory.

   Led by these signs and by these instances   219
Some have affirmed that bees possess a share
Of the divine mind and drink ethereal draughts;
For God, they say, pervades the whole creation,
Lands and the sea's expanse and the depths of sky.
Thence flocks and herds and men and all the beasts
Of the wild derive, each in his hour of birth,
The subtle breath of life; and surely thither
All things at last return, dissolved, restored.
There is no room for death: alive they fly

To join the stars and mount aloft to Heaven.   227

   Whenever you open up the stately home
Unsealing the honey stored in its treasure-chambers,
First draw a little water to douche your face,
Then hold before you a torch with searching smoke.
(Twice in the year men gather the honey harvest:
First when Taÿgetê the Pleiad shows
Her comely face to the world and with her foot
Has spurned the streams of Ocean, and again
When the same star, fleeing the rainy Sign
Of the fish, more sadly hastens down the sky   235
Into the wintry waves.) The rage of the bees
Is boundless: hurt, they breathe into their stings
Poison, and fasten on your veins to leave
Their secret javelins, and in that wound
Lay down their lives. But if you fear the harshness
Of winter, anxious to protect their future,
Pitying their bruised spirits and shattered fortunes,
Still, no one will forbear to fumigate
The hive with thyme and cut out empty cells;
For often an undiscovered newt has nibbled   242
The comb, and skulking woodlice that infect
The dormitories and the squatting drone
That brings no contribution to the mess;
Or the savage hornet with superior weapons
Has fought his way in, or the dreaded tribe
Of woodworms; or Minerva's hate, the spider,
Has draped the doors with her sagging hunting-nets.
The more the detriment, the more will prove
The keenness of each bee to set to work
And mend the wreckage of the ruined home,   249
Fill up the rows and fashion flowery store-rooms.

   But, seeing that life has brought to bees as well
Our human troubles, it may be that their bodies
Will droop with sad disease. When this occurs

You'll recognize it by the plainest symptoms.
The sufferers first change colour, and their aspect
Grows haggard and ugly. Then the living carry
The corpses of the lifeless out of the home
In funeral procession; or the sick
Hang at the entrance clustered by their feet,   257
Or shut indoors all moon about the house,
Listless with hunger and paralysed with cold.
A deeper sound is heard, a long-drawn buzzing;
As sometimes in the woods a chill south wind
Rustles, as ebbing waves of a rough sea
Wash on the shingle, or as hungry flames
Seethe in a shut-up furnace. In such cases
I advise the burning of fragrant fumes of gum
And honey introduced through pipes of reed:
Coax them yourself out of their listlessness,   266
Inviting them to their familiar fare.
Dried rose-petals flavoured with pounded oak-gall
Will also help to rouse them, or a mixture
Of must well thickened over a strong fire
Or syrup made from Psythian raisin-bunches
With Cecrops' thyme and pungent centaury.
There is also a meadow-flower that farmers call
Amellus. You will find it easily,
For from a single clump it pullulates
With a mass of stems; the disc itself is golden,   274
But in the abundant petals round about
Crimson is shot with violet. The altars
Of the gods are often decked with garlands of it.
Its taste is bitter. Shepherds gather it
In the cropped glens by Mella's winding banks.
Boil up the roots of this with scented wine
And place the food in baskets at the doors.

   But it can happen that a man has lost
His whole new generation suddenly
And knows no means to renovate his stock.   282

Now therefore is the moment to reveal
The Arcadian master's memorable resource,
How often in the past the putrid blood
Of slaughtered cattle has engendered bees.
I will unfold the legend, tracing it
In every detail to its very source.
Where favoured Macedonian colonists
Dwell at Canopus by the wide expanses
Of the Nile's flood and sail about their fields
In painted skiffs, and where the neighbouring frontiers   290
Of quiver-bearing Parthians impinge,
And where the river in its long descent
Right from the swarthy Ethiopians
Splits, hastening to seven separate mouths,
And with black sand makes fertile Egypt green,
There all the land relies on this device.
   First, for a site, a narrow spot is chosen
Confined for the very purpose. This they enclose
With a little tile-roof and constricting walls.
Four windows, opening to the four winds,   298
Admit a slanting light. Then next is sought
A bullock with two years' growth of curving horns.
Both nostrils and the life-breath of his mouth
Are plugged, for all his struggles. Finally
He is beaten to death, and with his hide unbroken
His flesh is pounded to pulp. In this condition
They abandon him shut up, with broken branches
Under his flanks and thyme and fresh-picked cassia.
All this occurs in the season when the Zephyrs
First ruffle the waves, before the fields begin   305
To redden with spring colours, and before
The chattering swallow hangs her nest from the rafters.
Meanwhile the moisture in those softened bones
Warms and ferments, and little animals,
An amazing sight, first limbless, then with wings
Whirring, begin to swarm, and gradually
Try the thin air, till suddenly, like rain

Shed from a cloud in summer, out they burst,
Or like a shower of arrows from the twang
Of bowstrings when swift Parthians start a battle.   314

Muses, what deity fashioned for us
This craft, or whence did this new human practice
Receive its impulse?
The shepherd Aristaeus, abandoning
Peneïan Tempê, so the story goes,
After the loss through famine and disease
Of all his bees, came and stood at the brink
Of the sacred river's utmost fountain-head,
Loud in complaint, and thus addressed his mother:
'Cyrenê, o my mother, dwelling there   321
Deep down beneath this pool, why did you bear me
For Fate to spurn, though sprung from seed divine
(If, as you say, my father is indeed
Apollo Lord of Thymbra)? What has banished
Your love for me? Why did you give me hope
Of immortality? Even this crown
Of my earthly life which skilful husbandry
Of crops and herds and every enterprise
Has hardly fashioned for me I must resign
Though having you for mother. Come, yourself   329
With your own hands root up my fruitful orchards,
Bring arson to my stalls, murder my crops,
Burn up my seedlings, wield a battle-axe
Against my vines, if you have grown so sick
Of what has been my pride.'
                              Within her chamber
In the river's depths his mother caught the sound.
Seated around, her Nymphs were spinning fleeces,
Milesian fleeces dyed with rich sea-green –
Drymo, Phyllodocê, Lygēa, Xantho,
Bright hair cascading over their white shoulders;   337
Cydippe and Lycorias the fair,
The one a virgin still, the other first

Newly acquainted with Lucina's pangs;
Clio and Beroë, daughters both of Ocean,
Both clad in dappled skins with golden girdles;
Ephyrê, Opis and Asian Deïopea,
And, now at last her arrows laid aside,
Swift Arethusa. Clymenê was telling
A story in their midst: the vain precautions   345
Of Vulcan were the theme, and Mars's trick
And stolen joys, and all the myriad loves,
From primal Chaos onwards, of the gods.
Charmed by her song they carried on unwinding
The soft wool from their spindles, till again
The plaintive cry of Aristaeus smote
His mother's ears. Then on their glassy seats
All were transfixed, till Arethusa first
Of all the sisters raised her golden head
To peer above the water, and from afar   352
Cried out: 'Cyrene, sister, not for nothing
You trembled at the sound of such a wail:
It is Aristaeus himself, your own beloved,
Standing in tears, denouncing you as cruel,
Beside the waters of our lord Peneüs.'
The mother, pierced to the heart by a strange fear,
Replied: 'O bring him here, bring him to us.
For him to tread the thresholds of the gods
Is no offence.' Whereat she bade the rivers
Part to admit the passage of the youth.   360
The waves like curving precipices reared
All round him, gathered him into the vastness
Of their bosom and sped him down beneath the flood.
    And now, marvelling at his mother's home,
The aqueous realms, the pools immured in caverns
And resonant groves, he moved, and in a daze
At the mighty motion of waters there beheld
All rivers gliding each in due direction
Under the massy earth – Phasis and Lycus,
The source from which the deep Enipeus bursts,   368

Whence Father Tiber, whence the Anio's streams,
The rocky, roaring Hypanis, Caïcus
Of Mysia, and bull-faced, with gilded horns,
Eridanus, than which no other river
More violently through fertile farmland flows
To join the dark blue sea. When he had reached
The chamber with its vault of pendant pumice
And when Cyrene had perceived those tears
Of her son were needless, duly her sisters brought
Water to wash his hands and well-shorn towels   376
To dry them. Some laid dishes on the table
And cups in turn refilled, while on the altars
Arabian incense flared. Then said his mother:
'Raise up your goblets of Maeonian wine
And pour in honour of Ocean'; and she prayed
Herself to Ocean, father of the world,
And to the sisterhood of Nymphs that guard
A hundred forests and a hundred rivers.
Three times upon the blazing, holy hearth
She poured a draught of nectar, and three times   384
The flame shot up and flickered on the roof
To cheer his heart with the omen. Then she spoke:
'In the Carpathian depths of Neptune's kingdom
Dwells Proteus, sea-green seer, who drives his car
Drawn by a team of three-legged, fish-tailed horses
Across the expanse of ocean. At this time
He is revisiting his place of birth,
Pallenê, and the Macedonian havens.
To him we Nymphs and even time-honoured Nereus
Pay reverence, for as a seer he knows   392
All that has been, is now, and lies in store,
For such is Neptune's will, whose monstrous herds
Of shapeless seals he pastures under sea.
Him you must catch, my son, and bind with fetters
If you would bring him to reveal the cause
Of this disease and prosper thus the issue.
For only by constraint will he give answer:

He bends to no entreaty; capture him
With ruthless force and fetters; only these
Will circumvent and shatter his designs.   400
And I myself, when the noonday sun has kindled
His hottest fire, when grasses wilt and shade
Is welcome to the herds, will be your guide
To the ancient's hiding-place, where he withdraws
When weary of the waves, that easily
You may assail him as he lies asleep.
But when you grasp him with your hands and hold him
In fetters, then in changing shapes and forms
Of beasts he'll baffle you; for suddenly
He'll be a bristly boar or a savage tiger   407
Or a scaly serpent or a lioness
With tawny neck, or burst with piercing hiss
As flame and slip his bonds, or melt away
Into unsubstantial water and be gone.
But the more he changes into myriad shapes
The more, my son, you must constrict his bonds
Till his body changes back into the form
In which you saw him newly fallen asleep.'
She spoke, and shed ambrosial scent around
To drench from head to foot her son's whole body,   416
Till from his smoothened hair a perfume breathed
Sweetness, and supple vigour braced his limbs.

    Within the side of a hollowed cliff there is
A spacious cave much visited by waves
Driven before the wind that split themselves
Into receding coves, at times affording
A perfect haven for sailors caught in storms.
Within this cave, under a mighty rock,
Proteus was wont to shelter. Here the nymph
Stationed the youth in ambush out of the light   423
And stood herself apart concealed in mist.
And now the torrid Dogstar's heat was scorching
The thirsty Indians, and the fiery sun
Had half consumed his course; the grass was arid

And gasping rivers, boiled beneath his rays,
Were shrunk into their beds and baked to mud,
When Proteus, leaving the waves to seek his cave,
Approached; around him the oozy denizens
Of the mighty deep cavorted, scattering
The salt spray far and wide. Anon the seals,   431
Sprawling about the beach, lay down to sleep.
Himself, like some lone herdsman in the mountains
When evening calls the cattle home from pasture
And bleating lambs provoke the hungry wolves,
Sat down on a rock in the midst and counted them.
Seeing the chance thus offered, Aristaeus
Scarce let the old seer settle his weary limbs,
But sprang upon him with a mighty shout
Surprising him with shackles where he lay.
He for his part, remembering his arts,   440
Transformed himself into miraculous shapes
Of every kind – a fire, a fearsome beast,
A flowing stream; but when no trickery
Won him escape, defeated he resumed
His human form, and thus at length began:
'Who then has told you, most presumptuous youth,
To invade my home? What do you want of me?'
'Proteus, you know it yourself,' said Aristaeus,
'You know full well, for nothing can deceive you;
So try no more deceit. Divine advice   448
Has sent me here to seek an oracle
For the revival of my flagging fortunes.'
So much he said. The seer, yielding at last
To strong compulsion, rolled his eyes ablaze
With sea-green light, and grumbling angrily
Unsealed his lips to utter Fate's decrees.

'The anger that pursues you is divine,
Grievous the sin you pay for. Piteous Orpheus
It is that seeks to invoke this penalty
Against you – did the Fates not interpose –   455

139

Far less than you deserve, for bitter anguish
At the sundering of his wife. You were the cause:
To escape from your embrace across a stream
Headlong she fled, nor did the poor doomed girl
Notice before her feet, deep in the grass,
The watcher on the bank, a monstrous serpent.
Then with their cries the Dryad band, her peers,
Filled the high mountain-tops. Mount Rhodope
Wailed, and Pangaea's peaks, and warlike Thrace,
The land of Rhesus, the Getae and the Hebrus   463
And Attic Orithuia. He himself
Sought with his lyre of hollow tortoiseshell
To soothe his love-sick heart, and you, sweet wife,
You on the desolate shore alone he sang,
You at return, you at decline of day.
Even the jaws of Taenarum he braved,
Those lofty portals of the Underworld,
And entering the gloomy grove of terror
Approached the shades and their tremendous king,
Hard hearts no human prayer can hope to soften.   470
His music shook them: drawn from the very depths
Of Erebus came insubstantial shades,
The phantoms of the lightless. Thick as birds
That hide themselves in thousands in the leaves
When evening or a wintry shower has brought them
Down from the mountains. Mothers were there and men,
And forms of great-heart heroes who had run
Their course; boys and unwedded girls, and youths
Laid on the pyre before their parents' eyes.
All these Cocȳtus circling round about   479
Hemmed in with pitchy mire and ugly sedge
And sluggish, hateful pools, and Styx itself
With nine-fold moat imprisoned. More than this,
The very halls of Death and inmost dens
Of Tartarus were awestruck, and the Furies,
Their dark-blue locks entwined with writhing snakes;
Cerberus stood with his three mouths agape,

[handwritten margin note: flees Aristaeus bitten by snake]

And the gale that drives Ixīon's wheel was stilled.
   At last, having evaded every hazard,
He was returning, and Eurydice   486
Restored to him and following behind
(So Proserpine's stern ruling had demanded)
Was coming back into the world above,
When suddenly a madness overcame
The unwary lover – pardonable indeed
Did Hell know any pardoning: he halted
And on the very brink of light, alas,
Forgetful, yielding in his will, looked back
At his own Eurydice. At that same instant
All his endeavour foundered, void the pact   492
Made with the ruthless tyrant; and three times
Thunder resounded over the pools of Avernus.
'Orpheus,' she cried, 'we are ruined, you and I!
What utter madness is this? See, once again
The cruel Fates are calling me back and darkness
Falls on my swimming eyes. Goodbye for ever.
I am borne away wrapped in an endless night,
Stretching to you, no longer yours, these hands,
These helpless hands.' She finished, and suddenly
Out of his sight, like smoke into thin air,   499
Vanished away, unable any more
To see him as he vainly grasped at shadows
With so much more to say; and the ferryman
Of Orcus would not let him pass again
Over the sundering marsh. What should he do,
Where turn, bereft a second time of her?
Would any weeping move the powers below
Or prayer the powers above? She all the while,
Now cold, was crossing in the Stygian barque.
   For seven whole months on end, they say, he wept   507
Beneath a lofty crag beside the Strymon
Alone in the wild, under the chilly stars,
And sang his tale of woe, entrancing tigers
And drawing oak-trees; as the nightingale

Mourning beneath the shade of a poplar-tree
Laments lost young ones whom a heartless ploughman
Has spied unfledged in the nest and plundered. She
Weeps all night long and perched upon a bough
Repeats her piteous plaint, and far and wide
Fills all the air with grief. No thought of love   516
Could touch his heart, no thought of marriage rites.
Alone he wandered over icy steppes
Of the farthest north, the snowy river Don
And those Rhipaean fields for ever wedded
To frost, lamenting for Eurydice
And Pluto's cancelled boon. But Thracian women,
Deeming themselves despised by such devotion,
Amid their Bacchic orgies in the night
Tore him apart, this youth, and strewed his limbs
Over the countryside. And so it was   523
That as the river of his fatherland,
The Hebrus, bore in the middle of its current
His head, now severed from his marble neck,
'Eurydice!' the voice and frozen tongue
Still called aloud, 'Ah, poor Eurydice!'
As life was ebbing away, and the river banks
Echoed across the flood, 'Eurydice!'

    So saying Proteus plunged into the depths
Churning a seething whirlpool where he plunged.
Cyrene stayed and of her own accord   530
Spoke to her shaken son: 'Now rid yourself
Of all your cares: the whole source of the plague
Lies in this story; this it was that caused
The nymphs with whom she used to dance her rounds
In the high woods to send this wretched blight
Upon your bees. You as their suppliant
Must sue with gifts for peace and venerate
These not unyielding spirits of the forest,
For they will grant you pardon as you pray
And will forget their anger. First however   536

I will teach you in what form to supplicate.
Four splendid bulls, outstanding in your herd
That now is grazing on Lycaeus' uplands,
Pick out, and likewise four unbroken heifers.
Set up four altars near those goddesses'
High shrines. On these let fall the sacred blood
Dripped from the severed throats, and then abandon
The carcases themselves in a leafy grove.
Later, when Dawn nine times has reappeared,
Pay poppies of forgetfulness to Orpheus   545
As funeral offerings, and sacrifice
A jet-black ewe. Revisit then the grove,
There worship with the slaughter of a calf
Eurydice, for she will be appeased.'
    Without delay he did his mother's bidding,
Came to the shrines and put in action there
The altars she prescribed, then brought to them
Four bulls superb in body and as many
Heifers whose neck had never felt the yoke.
Then, after the ninth rising of the dawn,   552
He returned to the grove. There suddenly is seen
A miracle: throughout the putrid flesh
Of the oxen's innards bees are buzzing, swarming,
Bursting from holes in the flanks, and trailing off
In a huge cloud to mass at the top of a tree
And hang in clusters from the sagging branches.

    This song of the husbandry of crops and beasts
And fruit-trees I was singing while great Caesar
Was thundering beside the deep Euphrates
In war, victoriously for grateful peoples   561
Appointing laws and setting his course for Heaven.
I, Virgil, at that time lay in the lap
Of sweet Parthenopê, enjoying there
The studies of inglorious ease, who once
Dallied in pastoral verse and with youth's boldness
Sang of you, Tityrus, lazing under a beech-tree.

Notes

BOOK I

2 *elms:* a small variety of elm was specially grown in a shape suitable to support vines.

5–23 See p. 28.

5 *brightest lamps:* sun and moon, invoked by Varro in his analogous list (*De Re Rustica* 1.1.5).

7 *Liber and . . . Ceres:* Roman equivalents of Bacchus and Demeter.

8 *Chaonia's:* in Chaonia (Albania) was Dodona, in whose oakgroves Jupiter had a famous oracle.

9 *Acheloüs:* in central Greece; reputed to be the oldest of rivers.

10 *Fauns:* Italian rustic deities who became associated with Pan (cf. Greek satyrs). *Dryad:* wood-nymph.

14 *Haunter of woods:* Aristaeus. It is strange that no reference is made here to his beekeeping, his only role, but a large one, in the *Georgics* (4.311–553).

19 *boy-inventor:* Triptolemus, prince of Eleusis near Athens, closely associated with the mystery religion there of Demeter.

24–42 See pp. 25–6.

28 *Venus' myrtle:* Venus was mother of Aeneas by Anchises, and thus (reputedly) of the Julian clan to which belonged Julius Caesar and, through his mother, this Caesar (Octavian).

30 *Thule:* land beyond Britain, not clearly identified.

31 *Tethys:* mother of the sea-nymphs, any of whom she might offer to Caesar in marriage (as Thetis was married to Peleus).

33 *a space:* in the zodiac the Virgin (Erigone or Astraea, symbolic of justice), presided over the period 20 August to 21 September, the Scorpion's Claws (alternatively Libra, the Scales, also symbolic of justice) over 22 September to 21 October. Virgil's conceit is, that the Scorpion is drawing in its usurping claws to make room for the star Caesar was destined to become (a Hellenistic mode of deification) in this suitable celestial locality. 23 September was his birthday.

39 *to follow Ceres:* the common version was that Proserpine, abducted by Pluto (Dis or Hades), was brought back by Ceres from the Underworld for six months of every year (when plant life revives on earth).

43 *early spring:* according to Varro (1.28) spring began officially in Italy on 7 February.

48 *twice:* the meaning of this passage was debated even in antiquity. Does it mean, plough twice in summer and twice in winter

144

(Pliny, *Naturalis Historia* 18.181) or by day for sun and night for frost (Servius *ad loc.*)? Both views have had modern supporters. The second ploughing was crosswise at right angles.

62 *Deucalion*: the Greek Noah, who, with his wife Pyrrha, re-peopled the world after the Flood by throwing stones that turned into human beings.

69 *choked with weeds*: Pliny (*Naturalis Historia* 18.242) disagreed: ploughing in early spring would only encourage weeds, which stifle the corn.

70 *moisture*: if Virgil is recommending a single furrowing (68) he is wrong. 'It is natural but erroneous to suppose that frequent stirring of the surface will deprive such soil of its moisture. On the contrary, by opening the pores it will arrest capillary action and help to conserve moisture' (K. D. White, *Proceedings of the Virgil Society*, 1967–8, p. 14).

71–83 Virgil has not made his connection of thought very clear here. It seems to be: allow your land to recover after harvesting either by fallowing or by alternation of crops, e.g. spelt with beans, vetches or lupines. Some crops are less suitable for this, e.g. flax, oats, poppies, for they parch the land. But no alternation of crops involves much labour, only manuring and burning, and there is the advantage over fallowing of the value of the crop itself.

78 *poppies*: poppy seeds were ground for oil, or used unground in cakes; also as a soporific (Pliny, *Naturalis Historia* 18.229), hence the reference here to Lethe, the river of forgetfulness from which the dead, on entering the Underworld, were supposed to drink.

84–93 *fire the stubble*: Virgil was under no obligation to speculate on scientific reasons for this; his doing so is reminiscent of Lucretius. As to his tentative explanations (no written source is extant), the 'mysterious' strength would now be explained by the small contribution made in nitrogen, phosphorus and potash; the 'noxiousness' would include viruses, disease spores and (he might have added) harmful insects. The third and fourth reasons are mutually exclusive, and neither of them plausible. Pliny (*Naturalis Historia* 18.300) adds a fifth and plausible one: killing the seeds of weeds. He also tells us (17.49) that the Transpadanes burned even stable dung to make ash fertilizer.

98 *angled*: this seems to be the meaning of *in obliquum*: the plough is driven down the same furrow but held at an angle to break down the ridge, the ancient plough having no built-in mould board.

121–46 *The Father himself* . . . : see pp. 28–9.

125 *Before Jove's reign*: the reign of his father Saturn (Greek Kronos), whom he supplanted, was the mythical Golden Age of natural abundance and slothful ease.

148–9 *acorns* . . . *Dodona*: see note on 8.

164 *threshing-sledges:* these had hard flints or iron teeth embedded on the underside, to release the grain from the straw.

165–7 *Celeüs:* father of Triptolemus (see note on 19). *Iacchus* (Bacchus) was important in the Eleusinian mystery religion. The 'winnowing-fan' (*vannus*) was a large osier basket.

169–75 For the plough see K. D. White, *Agricultural Implements of the Roman World* (1967), pp. 123–45, with figure on p. 129.

207 *Abydos:* on the Asiatic shore of the Hellespontic narrows (now Chanak).

208 *Libra:* the sign of the Scales in the Zodiac (see note on 33). It balances night and day at the autumnal equinox.

218 *the dazzling Bull:* the sun enters Taurus on 17 April. Virgil's wording suggests the bulls with gilded horns that were sacrificed at Roman Triumphs. The Dog-star is Sirius.

221 *Pleiads:* daughters of Atlas; Maia is one of them. Their morning setting is on 11 November.

222 *Cnossian Star:* the crown of Ariadne of Cnossos in Crete, set in the sky by her lover Bacchus.

226 *wild oats:* it was believed that corn left too long in the ground sprouted as wild oats.

228 *Pelusian:* Pelusium was in the Nile delta.

231 *This is the reason why:* the word (*idcirco*) relates the preceding and following passages to teleology, and so to Providence (see 238).

233–9 *Five zones . . . :* this passage is based on one by Eratosthenes, the third-century Alexandrian scholar-poet. Virgil speaks of zones of the sky, envisaged as corresponding to those on the earth. The earth is conceived of as stationary in a circumambient sky which is elongated to a peak at the north and south, directions somewhat confusingly indicated by reference to earthly geographical regions. The southern peak (nadir) should be visible to the antipodeans; how it could be visible to the Underworld of the Styx and the dead (Orcus, Tartarus) is not clear. In fact science is here being invaded by mythology.

239 *obliquely:* the sun's ecliptic, which crosses the Equator at an angle of 23½ degrees.

244–6 *Serpent:* the constellation Anguis lies between the Great and Little Bears. These stars, near the Pole Star, never 'sink beneath the Ocean', i.e. set, to the Mediterranean observer. Line 246 is ultimately Homeric.

249 *brings back day:* it is strange that Virgil could conceive of the possibility that when it is day here it could be night in the southern hemisphere and *vice versa*; but this enabled William Pitt to apply lines 250–51 to Europe and Africa with splendid effect (see p. 48).

265 *Amerian:* Ameria in Umbria was famous for willows.

280 *brothers:* the brothers Otis and Ephialtes, sons of Aloeus.

299 *strip . . . :* the quotation is from Hesiod.

305–6 *acorns:* used for pig-food. Berries of bay and myrtle were used for flavouring.

343–50 *worship Ceres . . . :* features of three festivals are here combined, the Cerealia (April), Ambarvalia (May) and a harvest festival of Ceres. Again we observe that Virgil was concerned with literature, not reportage.

343 *farmhands:* these would include hired labourers, with neighbours to help out, at busier times, at least on a larger holding.

363 *cormorants:* Virgil says 'sea coots', non-existent birds.

370 *Boreas:* the north wind. *Zephyrus* was the west, *Eurus* the south-east (or east).

379 *Her eggs:* from Aratus; but actually it is grains of corn that she brings out.

384 *Caÿster:* the river of Ephesus.

399 *halcyons:* mythical birds, reputed to nest on the sea. During fourteen days of winter when they brooded it was calm; hence 'halcyon days'. Virgil's idea is convoluted: it is a sign of calm weather when halcyons need no longer be on shore to sun their wings. The word 'halcyon' was also used for the kingfisher, as at 3.338. In myth Alcyone, when her husband was shipwrecked, threw herself into the sea and was turned into a kingfisher (Ovid, *Metamorphoses* 11,384 f.).

403 *in vain:* the idea is that the owl's hoot is a call for rain: it is now being frustrated.

404 *Nisus:* king of Megara. His daughter Scylla fell in love with Minos, who was besieging the city, and cut for him from her father's head the lock on which his life depended. She was changed into a sea-bird called 'ciris', Nisus into the sea-eagle, who relentlessly pursues her. There is a poem about her story in the *Virgilian Appendix.* Cf. Ovid, *Metamorphoses* 8.8 f.

409 *cleaves the air:* Virgil's repeated line conveys that she flies straight on – her best hope (relying on his dropping behind through missing his stoop).

418 *Jove:* here equivalent to the sky.

428 *dusky air:* if the crescent moon is very bright, its horns appear to embrace dusky air. Really this is the rest of its orb dimly lit by reflection of its own beams from the earth. T. E. Page quotes from the Scottish ballad of Sir Patrick Spens:

> I saw the new moon late yestreen
> Wi' the old moon in her arms.

431 *Phoebe:* the Moon as sister of Phoebus Apollo, the Sun.

437 *Glaucus, Panopea and Melicertes:* this line of sea-deities' names is modelled on a Greek one by Parthenius, a former prisoner of war who is said to have taught Virgil Greek.

447 *Aurora:* or Eos, Dawn. She asked Zeus for immortality for her husband Tithonus, but forgot to include agelessness.

467 *lurid gloom:* fanciful portents apart, there does seem to be evidence that the months after Caesar's murder witnessed unusual obfuscation of the atmosphere.

471 *Cyclopses:* giants who forged Jupiter's thunderbolts on Etna.

482 *Eridanus:* or Padus, the Po.

490 *a second time:* the first battle was that between Julius Caesar and Pompey at Pharsalus in Thessaly, some distance from the site of the second, Philippi in Macedon, but Virgil did not let that stand in the way of rhetoric; indeed his grasp of geography sometimes seems to be far from sure. *Emathia* is loosely used for the area of Macedon and Thessaly; and *Haemus* is actually a Macedonian mountain massif.

498 *Heroes of our land: Indigetes,* ancient Roman deities of mysterious identity. According to Festus (*Paulus* 106M) their names might not be made public. Aeneas became one, according to Virgil, *Aeneid* 12. 794; cf. Livy 1.2.6.; so 'Heroes', i.e. deified benefactors, may be as near as we can get to a translation: The *Gods of our fathers* may be those whom Aeneas brought from Troy.

499 *Tuscan:* the Tiber flowed through Etruria; but the word also recalls Rome's early Etruscan phase. The *Palatine* was the first of Rome's seven hills to be inhabited.

500 *Laomedon:* king who cheated Apollo and Neptune of their promised reward for building the walls of Troy. To the generation of the civil wars it seemed as if Rome must be under some primal curse; and Horace (*Odes* 3.3.21–4) followed Virgil in using Laomedon's legendary perjury as a symbol for the original sin of the race.

509 *Euphrates:* stands for the Parthians, a long-standing threat to the Roman Empire.

511 *Impious:* because fratricidal. To call Mars, the god of war, impious is a bold, paradoxical conceit.

BOOK 2

4; 7 *Father of the Winepress:* Lenaios was a Greek name for Bacchus.

9–34 *various:* variety characterizes this Book. Virgil distinguishes two methods of propagation: (1) wild (10–21), subdivided into (a) spontaneous, (b) from fallen seed, (c) from a root; (2) cultivated (22–34), subdivided into (a) suckers, (b) stakes, (c) layers, (d) slips from high up, (e) sawn trunks, (f) grafts. He changes the order of *Theophrastus (Historia Plantarum* 2.1f.) so that the inward eye of the reader travels upwards. Two of the ideas are chimerical: that plants can spring 'spontaneously' without seed, and that grafts can succeed between members of different families (cf. 69–72; 76; 82). As to the latter at least, Pliny knew better (*Naturalis Historia* 17.103).

15–16 *Jove:* Zeus of Dodona in Chaonia; cf. 67 and note on 1.8.

18 *Delphic:* on Parnassus, the mountain of Apollo and the Muses. Poets were crowned with bay.

26 *layers:* offshoots bent over and pegged into the ground unsevered from their parent.

37–8 *Ismarus*, or *-a*: a mountain in Thrace with bacchic associations. *Taburnus:* a mountain near Virgil's home at Naples. He likes to couple places in the Greek world famous in myth, song or history with familiar Italian places.

43 '*Not if I had . . . :* from Homer, *Iliad* 2.488 ff.; cf. Ennius, *Annals* 561–2.

49 *power: natura*, cf. 11; in modern terms, chemical action.

51 *trained:* an individual tree, transplanted to better conditions and properly tended, can produce better fruit. New and permanently improved varieties ('cultivars') can be produced by progressively selective breeding, perhaps with crossing of promising specimens – a long process unless luck produces a favourable mutation.

67 *Hercules:* when he brought up the monstrous dog Cerberus in triumph from the Underworld.

87 *Alcinoüs:* for the orchards of this mythical king of Phaeacia see Homer, *Odyssey* 7.112 f.

89–102 The first known discriminatory wine list. Julius Caesar prescribed Mamertine (from Messina) for public feasts. Augustus favoured Sentinan, Maecenas Caecuban, Horace Falernian. Lesbos and Thasos are islands in the north Aegean, Mareotis a lagoon at Alexandria. Rhaetic, liked by the elder Cato but not by Catullus, came from north Italy, the Aminnean from Picenum, the Falernian from Virgil's own Campania. Tmolus is the mountain of Sardis in Asia Minor.

115 *Gelonians:* from South Russia. *Saba:* south Arabia, sometimes identified with the Sheba of the Old Testament.

119 *acacia: acanthus* here seems to be, not our plant of that name, but the Egyptian acacia, which produces gum and has pods (not berries).

121 *silk:* believed at that time to be a vegetable product.

127 *citron:* its juice, mixed with wine, was emetic, according to Virgil's source, Theophrastus.

140 *bulls:* the mythical fire-breathing bulls yoked by Jason for the sowing of the dragon's teeth, from which sprang warriors he had to kill. The point is that Italy has no horrific myths.

143 *Massic:* Massicus is a mountain in Virgil's Campania.

146 *Clitumnus:* a beautiful river in Umbria, with a shrine of Jupiter at its source, where the cattle were bred for Roman Triumphs.

150 *Twice:* in fact only a rare phenomenon in either case; but this is panegyric.

151–4 *are not found:* their absence typical of the Golden Age; cf. *Bucolics* 4.22–5. Monkshood (*aconita*) has perplexed, since it is known to have grown in Italy. J. Sargeaunt suggested that this was the poisonous pale yellow monkshood, which deceived by its resemblance to the harmless aconite.

158 *Upper, Lower:* 'Mare Superum' (Adriatic) and 'Inferum' (Tyrrhenian).

159–60 *Lárius* is Como, *Benācus* is Garda.

161 *Lucrine:* in 37 B.C. Agrippa constructed the Portus Julius near Virgil's home: he replaced with a mole the sea-bank that shielded the Lucrine Lake from the Gulf of Naples, to baffle the waves, and pierced it to admit shipping, and further pierced a mile of land to connect the Lucrine with Lake Avernus, thus creating an outer and an inner harbour.

165 *mines:* panegyric exaggeration again.

169–70 *Marii, Camilli:* i.e. men such as Marius and Camillus; likewise the elder and younger Scipios and Caesar, i.e. Octavian.

172 *Unwarlike Indians:* this is what Virgil actually says; but it was the Parthians, not the Indians beyond them, that Caesar was facing; and to call an enemy 'unwarlike' is to belittle a commander. Some more generally pejorative phrase seems to be called for, such as 'base Orientals'. *Roman strongholds (arces):* it is not clear whether Virgil has in mind frontier posts or, by exaggeration, Rome itself.

176 *song of Ascra:* i.e. a Roman counterpart to the *Works and Days* of Hesiod of Ascra.

196 *goats that damage plants:* the bite of the goat in particular was believed to be poisonous; cf. 378 ff.

198 *hapless Mantua:* it had land confiscated for settling veterans after the Battle of Philippi. See *Bucolics* 9 and 1 and p. 14.

214–16 *Claim (negant alios aeque):* presumably ironical.

225 *Clanius:* a Dantesque touch. The flooding of Acerrae by this river near Virgil's Campanian home must have impressed him. Capua and Vesuvius are also in that neighbourhood.

229 *Lyaeus:* yet another name for Bacchus, perhaps introduced simply to dignify a particularly down-to-earth passage.

304 *oily bark (pinguis):* untrue, for the bark of olives is not particularly inflammable.

320 *white bird:* the stork.

325–7 The fertilizing marriage of Sky and Earth was an age-old idea; cf. Lucretius 1.250–61. The Virgilian concept of the earth as sentient is most operative in the passage that follows.

336 *dawn of the infant world:* the idea that the world began at the vernal equinox came from Greco–Egyptian astrology. Cf. Dante, *Inferno* 1.37.

350–3 *covered:* but the words Virgil uses (*super urgerent*) suggest pressing down, an impossible idea.

381 *staging of plays:* the Athenians, Theseus' sons, evolved tragedy (connected with *tragos*, goat) from performances at festivals of Bacchus (Dionysus). Virgil seems also to have thought that comedy was named from *kōmē* (village) rather than *kōmos* (a band of revellers).

384 *greasy goatskins:* the game was to see who could balance longest on a slippery bladder made from the sacrificed goat.

385 *Ausonian:* used by Virgil for 'Italian'.

385 *pilgrims:* the founders of Rome who accompanied Aeneas from Troy are represented as having had a mission (*gens missa*). The festival described seems to have been the Compitalia, celebrated at crossroads for the Lares but here approximated (? after Varro) to the Attic Dionysia – hence the connection with Bacchus.

407 *Saturn:* regularly represented at Rome with a hook in his hand.

410 *Twice:* vines must be trimmed first to remove the tops of shoots which might otherwise develop at the expense of the fruit, then to let the sun ripen the grapes.

412 *'Praise . . . :* adapted, after Cato, from a saying of Hesiod (*Works and Days* 643) about ships.

418 *stir the dust:* probably to mantle the grapes as protection against excessive sun or fog (cf. Columella, *De Arboribus* 12); but some take it to refer to piling dust round the roots.

438 *Cytorus:* in Asia Minor. *Naryx* or Narycus is in the 'toe' of Italy (see note on 37–8).

446 *osiers:* used to make fences and baskets; elm leaves were for fodder.

455–7 The famous battle of the Centaurs and Lapiths, inflamed by wine at a wedding feast, which is depicted on the Parthenon metopes in the British Museum and on a pediment of the temple of Zeus at Olympia. Line 457 may have been suggested by a work of art.

462 *morning callers:* the clients whose numbers were a status-symbol for the great at Rome.

469 *Tempê:* Tempe is a gorge in Thessaly, a famous beauty-spot.

474 *Departing Justice:* in the myth of the declining ages of man the departure of Justice signalled the final prevalence of the Iron Age.

475–82 Virgil will have attempted scientific study when he was in the Epicurean school of Siro at Naples.

484 *blood about the heart:* Empedocles, the Sicilian poet-philosopher of the fifth century, located the seat of thought in the blood surrounding the heart.

490 *Blessèd is he (felix*, a strong word): primarily Epicurus, but verbal reminiscences show that Virgil has Lucretius in mind; e.g. Acheron, cf. Lucretius 3.37. The wailings heard on this river of the Underworld stand for man's fears of the afterlife.

495 *fasces:* the bundles of rods, symbol of authority, carried by the consul's lictors; adopted by Mussolini as the emblem of 'Fascism'. Cf. Lucretius 3.996.

497 *Dacian tribesmen:* living in what is now Romania.

498 *crumbling kingdoms:* topically, of Asia Minor and Egypt.

502 *public archives:* the *tabularia*, on the side of the Capitol overlooking the Forum.

513 *The farmer cleaves . . . :* with impressive suddenness Virgil repeats almost exactly the slow, stable line he used at 1.494 of the farmer on the field of Philippi contemplating ages later the bones of dead soldiers he has turned up.

533 *Remus:* here and at Aeneid 1.292 Virgil tacitly puts aside any thought of the legend that Romulus killed his brother.

536 *Dictaean Jove:* Jupiter was said to have been born in a cave on Mount Dicte in Crete.

537 *slaughtered oxen:* the ancients had a certain guilt-feeling about killing their fellow-labourer for food. In Aratus it was the men of the Age of Bronze who first did this. Ovid elaborates the theme at *Metamorphoses* 15.111 ff. Cf. Varro, *De Re Rustica* 2.5.4.

538 *golden Saturn:* Saturn, equivalent of the Greek Kronos who was deposed by his son Zeus-Jupiter, is here merged with the old Italian god of sowing, Saturnus, who reigned in Latium, the district round Rome: cf. 2.173 and Varro 3.1.5.

BOOK 3

1–2 *Pales:* an Italian agricultural deity, generally thought of as feminine. *Amphrysus:* a river in Thessaly beside which Apollo 'the Shepherd' (*Nomios*) kept the flocks of Admetus.

4–8 *Eurystheus:* Greek king who, at Juno's instigation, imposed the Twelve Labours on Hercules. *Busiris:* Egyptian king who sacrificed strangers. *Hylas:* Hercules' page, drowned by nymphs. *Delos:* the Aegean island where Latona bore Apollo and Diana. *Hippodameia:* won as bride by Pelops' cheating in a chariot-race. When he was served up as meat to the gods by his father Tantalus they detected the fraud in time to save his life, replacing in ivory his shoulder, which had already been eaten by Ceres.

9 *'fly victorious . . . :* adapted from the epitaph composed for himself by Ennius, the first great Roman poet.

10–39 See General Introduction, p. 24.

12 *Idumaean:* Syrian.

15 *Mincius:* the 'smooth-sliding' river that flows out of Lake Garda past Virgil's Mantua and into the Po.

24 *the change of scenes:* literally, 'how the scene disappears as the facets revolve' (of scenically painted triangular prisms).

24–33 Recent events. Some orientals fought at the naval battle of Actium in 31 B.C. for Antony and Cleopatra against Caesar. There was a suggestion at this time that Caesar should take the name Quirinus, another name for Romulus, to signify that he was the second founder of Rome. The Nile here symbolizes Cleopatra's hordes. After the subsequent capture of Alexandria Caesar made a military demonstration in the East (Niphates is in Armenia). The enemies defeated on the 'two utmost shores' are probably the Morini on the English Channel and the Bastarnae on the Black Sea. In August 29 Caesar celebrated a triple Triumph, for Actium, for Alexandria, and for victories elsewhere.

25 *rising:* in the Roman theatre the curtain was raised, not lowered, at the end of a scene. The inwoven figures seemed themselves to be raising it. The plays were a feature of Roman, not Greek, games, such as were held at this time for the consecration of the temple of the Divine Julius.

35–6 *Assaracus, Tros:* patriarchal kings of Troy.

37–9 *Envy:* presumably of Caesar and of the poet himself. *Cocytus:* the river of wailing in the Underworld. *Ixion:* bound there to an ever-turning wheel (by snakes, according to this version). The *rock unmasterable* was rolled there by Sisyphus up a mountain; each time he neared the summit it fell back again.

43–4 *Cithaeron:* mountain near Thebes, famous for hunting and for bacchic revels, as was Taÿgetus, near Sparta. Epidaurus is south-east of Corinth.

48 *Tithonus:* brother of Priam, a type of longevity. His wife Aurora obtained her prayer that he should be immortal, but forgot to include agelessness.

50 *The champion cow:* as elsewhere, Virgil changes abruptly to the matter-of-fact after a high-flown passage.

61 *four years:* late, by our standards.

90 *Cyllarus:* a horse entrusted by Juno to her stepson Pollux for training.

93 *Saturn:* father of Jupiter who, caught by his wife with his mistress Phillyra, turned himself into a horse and so fathered the centaur Chiron.

113 *Erichthonius:* an ancient king of Athens.

115 *Lapiths:* see note on 2.455–7.

123–37 *With this in mind . . . :* Virgil does not intimate that he is now turning from horses to cattle; but this is confirmed by the fact that the precepts on feeding come from Varro's section in *De Re Rustica* on cattle, and threshing-time was when cows were mated (horses, in spring).

140–2 Again Virgil is less than clear: waggons were drawn by cows, but it would be mares that dashed about the countryside, so the distinction has been made clear in the translation.

145–51 The scene is Lucania, near the 'heel' of Italy. Silarus and Tanager are rivers, Alburnus a mountain.

153 *Inachian Io:* Juno, jealous of Jupiter's love for Inachus' daughter Io, turned her into a cow and sent the gadfly to plague her.

158 *brand:* the object has been much disputed; probably it was to establish pedigree rather than ownership.

190 *three-year-old:* again rather late, by our standards.

224–41 This drama is a creation of Virgil's imagination, sparked off perhaps by a passage in Aristotle which he seems to have been reading (*Historia Animalium* 6.21).

260–3 The first reference in extant literature to Leander of Abydos, who used to swim the Hellespont by night to come to his love, Hero of Sestos. Undeterred by a storm which extinguished the beacon she lit to guide him, he lost his way and was drowned; she then killed herself.

267–8 *Venus:* Various reasons were alleged for Venus' anger with Boeotian Glaucus, whose chariot-team she maddened.

271–82 The idea that a mare could be impregnated by the wind is found already in Homer (*Iliad* 16.150; 20.223). The phenomenon was reported from various countries and almost universally credited, though it is no doubt simply a fancy, metaphorical of the swiftness of horses. The idea that mares do not run eastward Virgil would find in Aristotle (*Historia Animalium* 6.18). 'Horse-madness' translates the Greek *hippomanes.*

291–3 *Parnassus:* mountain of the Muses (like Helicon in Hesiod's Boeotia). Castalia is the fountain of poetic inspiration on its lower slopes, near Delphi. The 'gentle slope' is the easy path of following poetic tradition.

295 *decree:* Virgil playfully uses a grand word associated with praetors' edicts.

304 *departing year:* the ancient year ended with February.

313 *sailcloth:* Varro simply says 'for nautical use'; he may have been thinking of ropes, and Virgil, misunderstanding, may even have meant clothing by *velamina.*

346–8 The military motif again. Virgil may have had particularly in mind the famous forced march of Gaius Claudius Nero in 207. When Hasdrubal crossed the Alps into Italy to relieve Hannibal, Claudius was reputed to have marched with his legions 240 miles in six days to relieve his consular colleague. Hasdrubal, waking to the sound of *two* trumpets from the Roman camp, realized that he was doomed.

351 *Rhodope:* a mountain massif in Thrace with a northward arc. Virgil's geography is vague and impressionistic.

388 *tongue:* some modern observations have tended to confirm this.

399 *iron muzzles:* perhaps even spiked. Contrast Virgil's solicitude at 176–8 for calves to be allowed to enjoy their mothers' milk.

400–3 Much debated lines. It seems most likely that, as de Saint-Denis thinks, the *calathi* are not jars of wicker but wicker-clad jars, a common sight in Mediterranean lands. The day's yield of milk, which would not 'travel' in the heat, is made into cheese the same evening for immediate consumption. The evening's yield, kept through the cool of the night, is taken by the herdsman before daybreak into town, or alternatively treated with a modicum of salt etc. and stored up for winter use.

441 *scab:* this is actually caused by a parasitic mite.

445 *dip:* this is prophylactic. The ointment described at 448–51 is for use if the scab has got hold. In Cato ointment is used as a prophylactic *after* shearing (96), in Varro *before* shearing (2.11.6–7).

461–3 The relevance is, the demonstration that opening such a vein does no harm.

470–566 For the Noric plague see Introduction, pp. 97–8. No doubt there had been an animal plague in that region within living memory, though it is not documented otherwise. The setting in a real locality serves to give a fortification of authenticity to the rhetorical portrayal.

486 *worship of the gods:* the horror is enhanced by realization that the gods themselves are powerless to ensure even their own sacrifices. Cf. 531–3.

513 *God blind the wicked:* variant of a stock apotropaic formula, wishing one's troubles on to one's enemies.

550 *Chiron:* the famous centaur. Virgil does not scruple to enhance his rhetoric at the expense of realism by the intrusion of legendary characters and a Fury from Hell. So Milton in his blindness recalled Thamyris and Homer, Tiresias and Phineus.

BOOK 4

1 *from the air:* the ancients believed that honey fell as dew from heaven (because bees avidly consume 'honey-dew', a sweet, sticky substance found on some leaves). This connects up with the belief that bees have a special share in the divine, hence 'heavenly'.

15 *Procne:* of Athens, wife of Tereus. To punish him for infidelity she killed their son and served him up as a meal to his father. Pursued, she was changed into a swallow (and her sister Philomela was changed into a nightingale). The chimney-swallow has a red patch on its throat.

21 *kings:* the ancients generally (with exceptions, notably Aristotle) believed the most conspicuous bee in the hive to be a male. The true facts were discovered by the Dutchman J. Swammerdam (1637–80), and not published till 1752.

28 *spread their wings:* actually the object is to let bees drink, not dry themselves, as Varro knew.

30 *smells:* bees have a strong sense of smell, through the eight terminal segments of their antennae. For protecting them against bad smells see 47–9.

35 *entrance narrow:* it is true that extremes of heat and cold are harmful to bees, but they protect themselves against these by their own system of thermostatic control through vibration of their wings. The narrowness is really to deter intruders.

38 *seal with wax:* actually not with wax. The paste (*propolis*) is gathered, not from flowers, but from tree-buds (Virgil was here misled by Aristotle). *entrances: oras,* rare form of *ora* (Richter; cf. 188 and Ennius, *Annales* 66).

42 *tunnelling:* untrue of honey-bees; true only of wild bees, the 'solitary', 'mason' and 'carpenter'.

47 *yew:* considered poisonous. *crab:* evil-smelling; applied to trees as a medicament.

50 *voice:* Aristotle was uncertain whether bees could hear. Apparently they are very sensitive to vibrations in the ground, but not in the air.

53 *Roam:* the first flights are actually for purposes of cleaning; the longer swarming is delayed, the better.

54 *sip the river's surface:* actually bees do not drink on the wing; see note on 28.

56–7 The successive references are to 'bee-bread' (pollen to feed the young), wax for the honeycomb, and honey itself.

62–6 It is not certain that pleasant smells positively attract bees, certain that these clanging sounds, though time-honoured in myth and practice, do not; see note on 50. *Mighty Mother:* Cybele, orgiastic Phrygian goddess.

67–85 The battle of two hives under their kings is a flight of fancy, though if a swarm tries to rob another hive the owners naturally resist. Bees do not fight on the wing.

72 *bugle's broken bray:* the queen ('king') does emit such a call, but she fights only a rival, in single combat within the hive.

74 *Stings sharpened:* a detail possibly due to misinterpretation of the bees' action in cleansing their antennae with their legs.

87 *handful of dust:* Varro (*De Re Rustica*, 3.16.30) recommends this for allaying swarming bees. Virgil, for his ulterior purposes, transfers it to fighting bees.

88–102 Developed by Virgil from a passage in Varro (3.16.18) about different kinds of bee and ways of distinguishing sick from healthy bees. His phrase used of the sick, 'as if dusty', may have suggested Virgil's odd simile of the dusty traveller, 96–8.

106–7 *tear their wings off:* surprisingly ruthless; to clip one wing is enough.

111 *Priapus:* garden-god, scarecrow and phallic fertility-promoter in one; originally worshipped especially at Lampsacus on the Hellespont.

125 *Tarentum:* Taranto. Virgil calls it 'the Oebalian citadel' because it was founded by Spartans, and Oebalus was a Spartan king.

127 *Cilician:* from Corycus, a city there. Pompey had settled Cilician ex-pirates in south Italy.

148 *later generations:* the Spaniard Columella, taking up the challenge, composed the tenth of his twelve books *De Re Rustica*, on gardening, in hexameter verse.

151 *Curētēs:* the legend was that Kronos (Saturn) began devouring his children because he knew that one of them was to depose him, but his wife hid the infant Zeus (Jupiter) in a cave on Mount Dictē in Crete. Some priests called Curetes drowned his cries by clashing their cymbals, and bees, attracted by the sound (but see note on 62–6), fed him with honey, the service referred to here.

153 *Alone:* Virgil conveniently overlooks wasps, hornets and ants.

158–69 There is division of labour in the hive, but in fact the same bee specializes successively in different tasks. Age is the determining factor, the older being provisioners, the younger (generally) builders (contrary to what Virgil says at 178–83, partly at least following predecessors). *initiate* (*educunt*): an anthropomorphic fancy.

164 *nectar:* by this Virgil must mean honey, not the liquid gathered by bees which we call 'nectar' and which is not turned into honey until it is deposited in the cells; for he apparently shared the ancient belief that honey was gathered as such directly from plants.

177 Virgil here calls the bees 'Cecropian', Cecrops having been a king of Athens (cf. 'Oebalian' at note to 125), because Athens is near Mount Hymettus, famous for bees.

194 *tiny pebbles:* Virgil took from some predecessor the false idea that bees ballast themselves with these in high winds.

197–202 Not surprisingly, the ancients did not know how bees reproduce. Few of them were aware that the leader is a mother (see note on 21), who is impregnated by the first to reach her of a crowd of drones pursuing her high in the air. (F. Huber discovered this in 1791.) The method Virgil fixes on to suit his book, that bees gather their offspring from flowers, is only one of several hypotheses mentioned by Aristotle (*Historia Animalium* 5.21).

207 *seventh summer:* actually even a queen sees five at most; a worker lives for about six weeks, or possibly a few months if born in autumn (J. Dzierzon, 1855).

211 *Hydaspes:* actually an Indian river, but Virgil thinks of it as belonging to the Median (Persian) empire. His geography is often vague.

212–18 It is true that if the queen dies the hive probably perishes; but Virgil has heroicized the process anthropomorphically.

219–27 See Introduction p. 29.

230 *douche your face:* to quench any sparks from the torch (the most likely interpretation, by F. R. Dale). The object of the operation is to smoke out the bees.

231 *Twice in the year:* May and November. This is possible where enough flowers are available. Lines 236–8 ('The rage . . . lay down their lives') would come more naturally before those that have been bracketed in the translation.

244 *no contribution:* i.e. like a man who comes to a bottle-party without a bottle. Contributory dining-clubs were common at Rome.

246 *Minerva's hate:* Arachne challenged Minerva to a spinning competition and was turned into a spider for her presumption.

250 *flowery:* Virgil says 'with flowers', meaning 'with wax derived from flowers'.

256 *funeral procession:* bees do at least throw out corpses, with other debris of the hive.

270 *Cecrops:* an early king of Athens.

278 *Mella:* a river near Brescia, not far from Virgil's Mantuan home. He may here be taking his mind off his authorities and recalling personal experience.

283–5 *Arcadian master:* Aristaeus, a ruler in Arcadia before he went to Ceos (see note on 1.14). The method, called *Bugonia* by the Greeks, is described at 295–314 below. Most ancient authorities, with the significant exception of Aristotle, believed in some form of it, despite the fact that it could never have succeeded if put into practice (cf. the riddle of Samson at *Judges* 14.8, whence the dead lion on Lyle's Golden Syrup tins). Bees hate carrion anyway. Perhaps it was always cheaper to buy new ones.

287 *Macedonian colonists:* from Pella, in Macedon, came Ptolemy, one of Alexander's generals, who inherited Egypt on the break-up of his empire.

287–90 The three extreme points of the Nile delta are here indicated: *Canopus* is the western. *Parthians:* Virgil, seldom careful of geography, says 'Persians'. At 293 he says 'Indians' for Ethiopians.

301 *plugged:* presumably to keep in the life principle, which is to pass into the emergent bees.

315 *what deity:* a purely rhetorical question: we have already been told at 283 that it was 'the Arcadian master'.

317 *Peneïan Tempê:* the gorge of Tempe on the river Peneüs in Thessaly was a famous beauty-spot, typical of a cool valley at 2.469. The nymph *Cyrene* was Peneus' daughter. Aristaeus' bitter plea takes its tone from Achilles' plea to his mother, the nymph Thetis, at *Iliad* 1.349 f.

323 *Thymbra:* near Troy, famous for its temple of Apollo.

334 *Milesian:* the fleeces of Miletus were proverbially fine.

340 *Lucina:* goddess of childbirth. Virgil characterizes some of the nymphs, probably just to vary his catalogue rather than with any ulterior significance.

345-6 *Vulcan:* the story of how Ares (Mars) was caught in bed with Aphrodite (Venus) by her husband Hephaistos (Vulcan) is told in *Odyssey* 8. (Virgil does not mention here the ruse by which he ensnared them: 266 f.)

371 *bull-faced:* rivers were emblematically so represented, and the horns of sacrificial bulls at Rome were gilded. Eridanus is the Po.

387 *Carpathian:* round the island of Carpathus, between Rhodes and Crete. *Pallēnê* is in Thrace, on the northern coasts of the Aegean.

388 *Proteus:* again the story is adapted from Homer, from Menelaus' consultation of Proteus at *Odyssey* 4.351 ff.

392 *Nereus:* a sea-deity, father of the Nereid nymphs.

412 *constrict his bonds:* we must not ask how this would help in the case of fire or water.

415 *scent:* in Homer (*Odyssey* 4.445) the scent is to overcome the stench of the seals, in Virgil it is to enhance Aristaeus' heroic quality.

455 *Far less:* reading *haudquaquam ad meritum*. The alternative reading *haudquaquam ob meritum* 'which you in no way deserve', gives inappropriate sense: to suggest that Aristaeus was comparatively innocent because Eurydice died by an accident, treading on a snake, while fleeing from his embraces undercuts the moral seriousness of the story, *magna luis commissa*, 'grievous the sin you pay for' (454).

467 *Taenarum:* in the extreme south of Greece, one of the fabled entrances to the Underworld.

469 *tremendous king:* Dis (Pluto).

471 *Erebus:* the Underworld, also called Tartarus or Tartara (482) and Orcus (502). (The Greek name Hades is not found in Latin.) Cocytus and Styx were among its rivers; also Acheron (2.492).

483–4 *Cerberus:* the three-headed dog that guarded the gate of the Underworld. *Ixion:* see note on 3.37–9.

485–7 In Hellenistic fashion Virgil speeds his narrative to its climax by conveying key events only by backward allusion: here the relenting of Dis and Proserpine and the condition they had laid down for Eurydice's return, that Orpheus should not look back at her until they were in the upper world.

493 *Avernus:* the volcanic lake near Naples, another fabled entrance to the Underworld, here probably synonymous with the Underworld itself.

502 *ferryman:* Charon, who ferried the souls of the dead across the final barrier, the Styx.

508 *Strymon:* a river of Thrace.

530 *of her own accord:* once Cyrene knew what deity, for what offence, had caused the bees' death, she knew how it could be placated. The act of appeasement would prove itself to be the means of begetting new bees, though this is implied rather than stated.

539 *Lycaeus:* a mountain in Aristaeus' own Arcadia.

544 *nine times:* at Rome sacrifices were performed nine days after a funeral.

561 *Euphrates:* see note on 1.509. This is the earliest statement of what was to be the Augustan imperial ideal. *Heaven:* see 1.21–42 and introduction, pp. 25–6.

564 *Parthenopê:* a poetic name for Naples.

565–6 These lines refer to the *Bucolics:* 566 repeats almost verbatim the first line of the First Eclogue. *Dallied (lusi):* a reminder not to take the *Bucolics* as a whole too seriously; but *with youth's boldness* probably refers not only to his pioneering Latin pastoral, but also to his courageous plea to the young Caesar for the evicted farmers conveyed by the tenor of that Eclogue as a whole.